I0573753

Edie
and the
CEO

MARY HUGHES

CRIMSON
ROMANCE
F+W Media, Inc.

Published by
Crimson Romance
an imprint of F+W Media, Inc.
10151 Carver Road, Suite 200
Blue Ash, Ohio 45242

www.crimsonromance.com

ISBN 10: 1-4405-6429-9
ISBN 13: 978-1-4405-6429-1
eISBN 10: 1-4405-6430-2
eISBN 13: 978-1-4405-6430-7

Dedication

To my wonderful editors, Jennifer Lawler and Nina Ricker. I'm awed by your wisdom and your generosity in sharing your marvelous ideas with me. Thank you for making this book the best it can be.

To my husband Gregg, who inspires me every day.

Chapter One

To: ThePrez@serenityrangers.com
From: ED@mythicmail.com
Subject: Internet Jokes

I loved your viola joke. Here's one about computers.
What's the difference between a computer and a trampoline?
You take off your steel-toes before jumping on the trampoline :)
—ED

Smack in the middle of the workday, because her brain was fried, Edith Ellen Rowan made her computer chirp *Old MacDonald.* Naturally that got her into trouble with The Bitch.

At first, Edie didn't even register the problem. Four sunny bars bee-booped before it hit her—her computer was playing a children's nursery song in an office full of conservative, nitpicky ears. Houghton Howell Enterprises was staid like an insurance company's gray suit (fun was something you had on the golf course, or once a year at the Christmas party, but never *ever* on the job).

"Suck it to shell." Edie hit the escape key. As ee-eye-ohhh died, she braced against the proverbial fan scattering the proverbial manure in the form of Bethany Blondelle, known to most of the company as The "B" if they were feeling kindly, adding the "itch" if they were not.

Shoulders hunched and breath held, Edie waited. She'd only been trying to motivate her people. Managing a team of programmers at HHE, a firm that sold innovative (read: expensive) solutions in accounting for large companies (read: deep pockets) wasn't easy. Her team members were getting as fried as she, and so she'd proposed the music-writing contest.

Nothing happened. Edie gradually relaxed.

The Star Spangled Banner burst lustily from Jack's cubicle next door. Edie groaned.

"What the HELL is that NOISE?" Bethany had her vocal caps lock on again. This would be bad. "Who's making all that racket? Edie? Edie!"

Edie face-palmed. The contest was supposed to be a bit of fun, not cause for Armageddon. She'd have preferred to ignore The B, but "Bethany" and "proactive" were so synonymous they were hyperlinked on Wikipedia.

Sure enough, a long leg popped through the opening of Edie's cubicle, followed by the lady herself in eye-bleeding red.

Bethany's fashion sense was from the DoMeHard channel. Her snappy skirts were hemmed just below her panty line. Today's suit also featured a plunging sweetheart neckline, a chunky citrine necklace getting suffocated in her Wonder-enhanced cleavage. Her long, sleek hair was dyed crayon yellow #6.

Edie looked down at her own lacy teal tee, navy pants and wool blazer and wondered if she was underdressed.

Nah.

"What is the meaning of this racket?" Bethany leaned on Edie's desk, looming over her. Invading personal space—"A" in the ABCs of corporate dominance.

"Project Pleiades. We had a month to deadline—until your good buddy Junior chopped that to a week."

"Respect, Edie. *Mr.* Howell, not 'Junior.'"

"I'll respect *Mr.* Pharaoh Howell when he respects the workers. That deadline is a nightmare. My team has been working twelve-hour days and more. I've tried to push back, but you know Junior. Only the Evil Overlord can buck him."

"Stop it." Bethany tossed her head, a fleeting remnant of the girl Edie once knew. "The issue is not our executives. The issue is that…racket." She waved her hand toward Jack's cubicle, where the anthem was on its final verse.

"Handling Stress 101, Bethany. Work on something else."

"Playing music on company time?" Bethany glared down her high-bridged nose. "Stupidity 101. You should listen to me if you want to go anywhere in this company." She pointed to her cleavage, fingertip disappearing to the first knuckle. "After all, my team's twice the size of yours."

"Bigger isn't better. It's all about how you use it." Edie grinned. "How about you run your team and I'll run mine?"

"You don't run your team." Bethany sneered. "They run you."

"It's called empowerment." Edie took pride in her outspoken team. She wanted her grandparents, hard-core sixties protesters, to be proud of her. They'd raised her from a little girl when her parents had died, and she loved them to pieces. "It's a proven management style."

Jack's computer shifted to *A Hundred Bottles of Beer*.

"Management?" One corner of Bethany's perfect lips curled. "The only management I see is *mis*-management."

"Ba-dum-bum." Edie was suddenly tired of the whole conversation.

And, as Jack's computer continued to tweet bottles down, doubt gnawed at her. It *was* quite a racket.

"Other people are trying to work." Bethany went for the kill. "Keep your hooligans under control or I'm going to have to tell Mr. Kirk."

Edie suppressed a moan. Of all the straight-laced overbearing big shots at HHE, Edward Everett Kirk, president and CEO, was the biggest, straight-laciest. Like laced corsets…naughty corsets in Kirk's competent hands—

"The way you two fight, it's only a matter of time before he gets fed up and fires you." Mme La B'itch drew a red-enameled nail across her slim throat.

7

Edie winced. "It's called 'corporate unfriending' now. And I couldn't help the janitor incident. Or the thing with the Super Soaker. Look, I'll talk to my people. Just cut us some slack, okay? We've been working ridiculous hours."

"Edie, you idiot. Has it ever occurred to you that your ridiculous hours are because of *you?*"

Them's fightin' words. Edie raised narrowed eyes. "I beg your pardon?"

Bethany leaned knuckles on the desk. "Only one kind of project manager confuses effort with efficiency: a bad one."

"Enough." Edie jumped to her feet, nearly head-butting Bethany. "Outside. Now."

"And freeze my butt off? Hardly." Bethany's nose was inches from Edie's. "You have absolutely no decorum, do you? That shouldn't surprise me, considering the hippies who raised you."

Edie lost it. "My grandparents were heroes! They fought for what they believed in, rallied at protest marches—"

"Pretty stories. Your grandpa was a long-haired unwashed bum. Your grandma wasn't much better than a free love hooker."

Edie snarled. "Now you listen here, you b—"

"If Mr. Kirk were here—"

"Mr. Kirk," a deep voice rang with power, "*is* here. And I want to know what, precisely, is going on."

*

To: ED@mythicmail.com
From: ThePrez@serenityrangers.com
Subject: Re: Internet Jokes

Dear ED,

Well, you've done it again. Just when another date fizzles and I'm laid low, when the fifth power play of the week pummels me black and blue, when and I'm at my wits' end and think I'll never smile again, your email pops into my inbox and I'm laughing. How did I ever get along without you?

I know we agreed at the start of our relationship that we'd stay anonymous-cyber-friends-with-benefits. But it's been a year since we met on that Colorado social site. I'd like to know you better. You shouldn't give out personal information over the Internet, so if I send you my phone number, will you call?

No, on second thought, never mind. I don't want to ruin our friendship.

I bought a DVD the other day. "3.14159 out of 5 stars!" was written on the box. I think it was pirated! (Pi - rated :D)

—Prez

Filling the opening of Edie's cubicle was a blood-red silk tie, snow-white shirt, and perfectly cut pinstriped suit—elegant packaging for the raw breadth of an exceedingly masculine chest.

Edward Everett Kirk.

Charleton Heston would have been jealous of Kirk's high forehead, straight nose, strong mouth and square jaw. The gleaming wingtips and foil-thin gold watch were just added insult. Mr. Ultra-Executive.

Except for a neat chestnut ponytail and square workman's hands.

Edie found those elements a startling…intriguing…*annoying* contradiction. She shivered, stifled it. Something about Kirk pushed all her buttons.

"Mr. Kirk!" Bethany smoothed her skirt. "I'm so glad you're here. Edie is totally out of control—"

"One moment. Edie." Kirk stepped into the cube and suddenly Edie couldn't breathe. His gaze bored into her like a silver-blue drill. "The whole department is rumbling over an out-of-tune rendition of *Hundred Bottles* and a cat fight. And whom do I find at the center of it? Edie Rowan."

Edie chewed her lip. "I know it looks bad, Kirk. But—"

"*Mr.* Kirk." Bethany sliced an evil little look at Edie. "Let me remind you, company policy requires that HHE officers be called by their courtesy titles, to show our *respect.*"

"Respect isn't ordered." Edie gritted her teeth. "It's earned."

"Mr. Kirk, it's high time you do something about her." Bethany jabbed a finger at Edie. "Not only was she at the center of this disturbance, she proposed this whole absurd contest."

"Contest?" Kirk's flashing eyes, in another man, might have been amused. "Edie. What contest would that be?"

Edie opened her mouth.

"She bet lunch," Bethany jumped in. "On the company credit card, if you can believe it. Lunch for any of her hooligans who—"

Kirk raised his hand. That was all it took to chop Bethany off mid-tirade. "Excuse me, Bethany. I asked Edie." His nod gave Edie the floor.

She was impressed despite herself. Which teed her off. It wasn't impressive, it was the Great Man allowing the Poor Servant to speak. Her chin kicked up. "My team needed a stress valve. We've been putting in twelve-hour days, and—"

"A project manager," Bethany chirped, "should make the project manageable."

"What are you, the Sphinx?" Edie said.

"Can't stand the truth? Bad manager, bad manager…"

Edie came around her desk so fast her curls snapped. Her head barely cleared Bethany's shoulders, but her blazing temper towered. "Can. It."

"I certainly won't—"

"You *will*—"

"Conference room. *Now.*" Kirk effortlessly sliced through their tirade. He strode away without a backward glance.

Edie exchanged a murderous look with Bethany. But they both trailed Kirk to the conference room.

As soon as Edie shut the door, Kirk whirled and snapped, "You two bicker like small children. You're managers. Act like it."

Edie jerked straight as if she'd been slapped. "Yes, sir. My apologies, sir."

"No sarcasm, please." His narrowed eyes could have sliced steel. "You're pushing the line already."

Bethany said, "If you ask me, she's not only pushing the line, she crossed it and rubbed it out after her."

"Nobody asked you," Edie and Kirk said at the same time. Edie gave him a surprised look.

He simply nodded. "You were explaining the music. Please continue."

Edie took a calming breath. She wasn't trying to get fired but tact wasn't her strong suit. Honesty was. "My team is working really hard with an impossible deadline. They were burning out. So I made up a little contest to re-energize them. I challenged them to write a music program before I did."

Bethany broke in with undisguised glee. "She should spend less time playing at programming and more time working at managing."

Kirk cut her out of the conversation simply by turning his shoulders on her.

Edie was grudgingly impressed. Not by the breadth of those shoulders. By Bethany actually shutting up. Although those shoulders, besides blocking Bethany's scowl, obliterated half the conference room. No. Not gaping at his shoulders, or his strong lithe body, or his clean, rugged jaw. Definitely not falling under the spell of the gleaming intelligence in his eyes... She slammed hers shut.

Only to drag in the scent of male heat and power instead.

She tried to stop breathing. Choked. Her eyes snapped open.

He was watching her, irises so bright they were almost silver. Steel blue, emphasis on steel—Kirk used his eyes the way other men used swords. That gaze made her want to cower, to run for cover…bed covers, rolling under them in the dark, hot and sweaty… She covered her face with both hands.

"Tell me the rest." His voice was a buzz of pleasure along her skin.

"There's not much more to tell, Kirk…I mean Mr. Kirk." She uncovered. "I needed a diversion for the team. It was perfectly innocent. If Jack's music had played after hours, no one would have cared."

"But it isn't after hours, is it?" Though Kirk's tone was gentle, his eyes, sharp and demanding, held her to a higher standard. "Other people work here, Edie. There are other people to consider, besides your team."

"It was just a song or two." Edie's cheeks heated. "No big deal."

"The whole department was ruffled and distracted. I felt it just walking through. Didn't you sense it, right in the middle as you were?"

"Um…eye of the storm?"

"Bethany was kind enough to inform you of the disturbance in person. Didn't you listen to her, even a little?"

"She was gloating, not informing!"

"Edie." He shook his head, sadly. "You haven't learned a thing about cooperation and compromise in the workplace, have you?"

Edie's blood drained. That killing tone of voice…this was it. She was going to get fired. Again. "Look, I'm sorry. I'm doing the best I can for my team. Sometimes that means I lose sight of the big company picture."

Kirk frowned, his silvery eyes mirrored surfaces, unreadable.

A lifetime's silence passed. Edie chewed her lip. She wanted to scream.

Through it all, muffled by the conference room's walls, Jack's computer cheerfully took down bottles of beer and passed them around.

Her lip was in tatters when Kirk's frown finally eased. "Very well. You have a choice."

Okay. Not fired yet. Though, from the wicked curl to his lips, she wouldn't like his "choice."

"There's a management seminar in LA on Monday. Either attend it, or..." His steely eyes finished the sentence for her. Attend the seminar or get in the unemployment line.

"What kind of choice is that?" Bethany's pinched face peeped around Kirk's massive shoulders. "A week of half-days at a gorgeous ocean resort? It's a fantasy vacation, not a choice."

"What's the catch?" Edie said.

"No catch," Kirk said.

"Right." Edie grimaced. "Since it sounds like I take it or leave—I'll take it."

"Excellent." He smiled.

His smile caught Edie off-guard. Sparkling white teeth and gently crinkled eyes zapped her for ten points of damage before she could even think of getting her shields up.

His smile widened.

Fry her motherboard. He even had a killer dimple in his left cheek.

Belatedly her shields raised. The teeth were probably capped. The dimple was...unfair.

"That's settled," Kirk said. "I'll pick you up at six forty-five tomorrow morning."

She blinked. "What?"

"Your seminar is on the way to my conference. I'm driving anyway so I'll drop you off. No sense wasting the company's money."

"You're driving from Colorado to California?" No catch? A two-day drive through the mountains *alone* with Edward Everett Kirk? Sealed in with those shoulders, that chest, that smile? *Huge* catch. "I can drive myself."

13

"You could." He stepped closer, so close she heard his tie rustle against his shirt, felt his heat. So close she could shut her eyes and lean forward and raise her face...she snapped straight. "But why should you, when I'm already driving?" His voice deepened. "Let me do this for you, Edie."

"Is that..." Her voice was breathy. She swallowed, tried again. "Is that an order?"

"An order." He sighed. "If I must. Now go home and pack."

"*Now*? But it's only Friday and my team—"

"Will be perfectly fine for a few hours."

"But what about Project Pleiades? The deadline—"

"Mr. Kirk!" Bethany wedged a sharp elbow between Edie and Kirk. "While Edie's gone, why don't I take care of her team?" She shoved.

Kirk was a mountain and didn't move, but Edie got drilled in the diaphragm. She managed to gasp, "Over my dead—"

"No need, Bethany," Kirk cut in smoothly. "I think they'd be best off without *both* of you for a while."

He smiled, unleashing the dimple. And while Edie stood stunned, he sauntered out.

Chapter Two

To: ThePrez@serenityrangers.com
From: ED@mythicmail.com
Subject: Re: Re: Internet Jokes

Dear Prez,

My grandma warned me against giving out my phone number on the web, so you shouldn't send me yours either. Unless you're a pervert? Then I guess it'd be all right :)

A year already since we met? Have you ever felt from the first moment you met someone that you've always known them? I feel like I've known you my whole life. Silly, when I don't even know your real name.

Two hydrogen atoms walk into a bar. One frowns and looks around. The other asks, "What's wrong?" The first says, "I lost an electron." The second asks, "Are you sure?" "Yes," the first replies. "I'm positive."

;)

—ED

Out of sight of the conference room, Everett massaged his temples. Pain sliced his skull behind his left eye, despite two extra-strength ibuprofen. His last girlfriend, who'd lasted all of three weeks, thought the headaches signaled an imminent stroke. She insisted he see a doctor. The wait for an appointment lasted longer than the girlfriend did—she broke up with him two days later.

Well, she'd always been more interested in his Lambo than him anyway.

The doctor told Everett he was suffering from stress. Surprise, surprise. Not only was HHE awash in stress—and carpeted, wallpapered and tastefully furnished in it—he'd become the rope in a corporate tug of war.

On one end was the mastodon of senior management led by Houghton Howell III, COO by way of being the son of the chairman and the founder's grandson. Most HHE senior management came up through Nepotism 'R Us. Not to say Howell Junior was out of touch with the worker, but he'd stepped right from his exclusive school into the executive wing and now played with management productivity tools in his air-conditioned corner office, shuffling positions on the company chart as if they were paper dolls instead of real people.

On the other end was a 110 pounds of Edie.

Despite his headache, Everett smiled. The day they'd met, she'd been filling the cafeteria napkin holder—backwards. When he told her she was doing it wrong, she calmly handed him the holder and told him to do the job himself. People laughed at her for treating him like a janitor, but none of them dreamed he'd done jobs even more menial to get where he was.

Edie was a beacon for employee rights—no, a bonfire. How appropriate that one small fireball of a woman balanced a whole org chart of self-entitled one-percenters.

Well, not balanced, exactly. Even with her fire, the tug of war would have been over long ago if the rope hadn't been secretly siding with her. She'd never know how many times he'd come to her rescue.

Pain stabbed Everett's brain, abruptly killing his smile. He detoured to a water fountain to wash down another pair of ibuprofen.

Hanging onto the basin, he willed the pain to recede. A good, brisk workout at his health club took care of his worst headaches, but he hadn't been there in weeks. Countering murderous rumors and sabotage had a way of eating into "me" time. And now he had to smooth Edie's path of self-righteous destruction yet again.

He massaged his aching forehead. She was the best team manager he had, but so young. True, he was only three years older, but he'd learned long ago that not everything could be solved by simply being right. Being effective was much more important.

Effective and quiet. In corporate America, the squeaky wheel didn't get the grease, it got the boot. Companies were like parents—they didn't care what you did, as long as you were quiet.

Hopefully camp would open up Edie's eyes. Her fine, dark eyes. His headache receded, thinking about those beautiful eyes. Thinking of them watching him as he drove through the mountains. Even fighting with her would be more fun than the boring, lonely trip he'd originally envisioned. With her sunny red curls, her lovely pink mouth, her pert breasts that bounced so prettily as she trotted down the hall...his groin tightened.

He didn't dare massage *that* ache away.

In fact, he hadn't taken care of that particular ache for some time. Thank you, grueling schedule. Nearly two years now since he'd had time for a relationship outside the company.

Although if he was honest with himself, it was also due to his standards. He wanted, not a bed buddy, but a companion.

Finding a mate for his corporate self wasn't a problem, not with so many board bunnies opening their, ahem, wallets. But he fiercely wanted a woman who could complement all of him— even the part he kept well hidden.

Edie's special light attracted that hidden side of him, nourished his secret self. She might not be the companion for Corporate Everett, but he'd wanted for some time to get to know her better anyway. If not for her prickles, he'd have made his move well before this. Well, prickles and the company policy of no fraternization.

He was of a mind to give it a try despite company policy. If, after management camp, she still worked here.

If he still worked here.

That brought his headache back. The enemy who was trying to oust him from HHE would gleefully use this latest mess as ammunition.

He pushed away from the water fountain. Resumed his usual purposeful stride, camouflage for the crippling headache. He'd find another job. But Edie…there was the rub.

Without him here to protect her, she was vulnerable. Blinded by her self-righteousness, she'd thrust her neck onto the corporate chopping block, unseeing until it was too late.

Picturing HHE without that fiery hair, that bouncing enthusiasm, that beacon of light… No. Unacceptable.

So. Goal: keep Edie at HHE. Dodge the attacks of the unknown enemy, stay president, get Edie to the seminar in one piece.

Hope she actually learned something and could begin to protect herself.

Savagely massaging his temples, he wondered which impossible task would prove hardest.

*

Blinded by his headache, Everett nearly ran into Bethany outside his office, tête-à-tête with a tall, classically handsome man whose red breast-pocket flourish and gold everything was overdone. Houghton Howell III, aka Junior. His father was technically Howell Jr. but with the founding Howell gone to the great stock market in the sky, Junior and Senior were more fitting for III and II.

Bethany shot Everett a triumphant look and sauntered away.

Delightful. She'd run straight to Howell then, to kick the confrontation up the ladder. Dear Bethany. Everett rather understood how she'd earned the vulgar nickname he wasn't supposed to know.

Well, better deal with this now, on his home turf. He nodded Howell into his office.

Howell neutralized Everett's advantage by planting butt in Everett's leather chair. For added insult, Junior kicked his feet onto Everett's desk.

Everett heaved a silent sigh. They'd been playing pinstripe apes since day one, beating chests and baring teeth in displays of corporate dominance. All because Everett was hired for the presidency Howell wanted. Everett was getting tired of it, but it went with the job. And he did his job damned well.

Crossing arms, he leaned against the wall, seemingly nonchalant though his head was killing him. "Comfortable, Howell?"

"Just getting used to the lay of the land, Kirk old boy. You're going soft, you know. You'd never have made a mistake like this in the early days, my friend."

"I don't recall making any mistakes, *my friend*. Enlighten me."

Howell smirked, the expression prissy on his narrow features. "The Rowan woman, of course. You need to fire her."

Everett shook his head. "She's our best manager."

"Best screw-up, you mean."

"No. I don't." Everett straightened away from the wall. "And it's my decision to make, not yours."

Howell studied buffed fingernails. "It may be mine in the future."

"Perhaps—but not today. Time's up, Howell." Striding to his desk, Everett poked Howell's heels off. They hit the floor with a thud.

"Fine." Howell stood. "You're president—for now."

"Exactly. *I'm* president." He let his anger show. "And Daddy's enterprises are profitable. That's all the board of directors cares about, Howell."

"Not all." Howell leaned forward, toe to toe and eye to eye, invading Everett's space.

Everett neutralized him by simply straightening to his full height and glaring down.

Howell backed off. A mean glint entered his eye. "You may top me in the org chart but the board tops you. I wonder whom *they* favor? Oh wait. We'll find out next month at the annual review meeting. My brass nameplate will look good on this desk, don't you think?"

He spun and left.

Everett closed the door quietly. They'd bared their teeth and beaten their chests, and Everett had won.

But in retaliation Howell had brought in King Kong.

*

To: ED@mythicmail.com
From: ThePrez@serenityrangers.com
Subject: About me

My real name. Well, my mom called me Ev, my college friends called me E.E., and the people at work call me Hardass—they don't appreciate my sterling qualities. Pick one ;)

Were you trying to electrify me with that last joke? Speaking of…How many programmers does it take to change a light bulb? None, it's a hardware problem.

—Prez

That night—after she'd told her MMO guild she'd be away from keyboard for a week—Edie got on a Skype session with her grandparents. She told them about the camp and why she was going—but *not* whom she was traveling with.

Yet her grandmother said, "Who is he?"

"He? There's no he." The heat in Edie's face said she was blushing like crazy but at 240p her grandparents wouldn't see it.

"Of course not." Fortunately her grandmother let it drop and they ended the call as they always did.

"I just want you to be proud of me," Edie said.

"We are, sweetheart. We are."

*

The next morning, the first thing to breach Edie's awareness was soft, soothing music from her clock radio.

Followed by loud, masculine swearing from her apartment door.

A startled glance at the clock told her she'd overslept. Jingling jump drives, Kirk was here to pick her up. Two days alone in a car with his authority, his shoulders, his *smile*—

Pounding blasted the door. The man had fists like sledgehammers. Something told her he'd been pounding quite a while.

She groaned. She hadn't even had her coffee yet. Thank goodness her brand-new, theft-deterrent door stood between her and a blistering lecture. She clambered out of bed and threw a robe over her oversized T-shirt. More pounding, blisteringly loud, drowned out the soft padding of her bare feet. Hopefully the door was as good as the sales rep promised.

She padded a bleary path from her bedroom, along the hall toward the living room.

The pounding stopped.

He'd given up. Yay. Not that Kirk was known for giving up, but she was desperate for caffeine. She U-turned for the kitchen.

A *bam* spun her. A *bang*, and the front door burst open in a shower of splintered wood.

Kirk rushed through. "Damn it, Edie. Are you all right?"

"Don't swear. Of course I'm all right. Why wouldn't I be all right?"

He stepped into her living room and she saw the damage. Her eyes opened wide. Both door and jamb were splintered.

Apparently the rep had overstated its solidness.

"I still have eleven easy payments left on that!" She scurried past Kirk to get a better look.

And stepped on a chunk of broken wood. "*Ouch.*" Pain slashed her sole, stabbed her big toe.

"Damn it, Edie. You should have slippers on."

"Please don't swear—"

"Screw that." Kirk swept down on her and scooped her up.

Her belly swooped. She'd been carried by a man once but not so effortlessly. Kirk's arms were immensely strong and secure and he smelled beguilingly of crisp air and cedar-packed wool. When he settled her on the living room couch, she was disappointed.

Disappointed? That scared the skit out of her. "I didn't need slippers. My floor was perfectly clean until a moment ago."

"We only have your word for that." He sat on the couch at her feet. Grabbing her injured foot, he pinched her toe.

"Yowch! What are you doing?"

"Removing a splinter. A big 'un."

"Sure you weren't trying to pop my toe off?" But it did feel better.

He lifted her foot. "Hmm. A couple gashes." He spread his arms to forklift her again. "We need to clean this."

"No, *we* don't." She ducked and scooted to one corner of the couch. "I can walk."

"Bare feet versus this floor? I'll carry you." He reached for her with his all-too-capable arms.

She leaped up, her injured foot slapping against hardwood. The gashes screamed protest and she stumbled, nearly face-planting into the wall.

Kirk leaped after her. "Damn it, Edie—"

"Language!" She palmed stop. "You're right. I'll keep it off the ground, see?" She lifted her foot high—pulling something in her groin. She winched down a grimace and bunnied one-legged into the hallway.

Out of sight, she cautiously set her foot down.

"If you risk infection by putting that foot down," Kirk called from the living room, "I will personally lash your ankle to your thigh. Let me warn you, I tie some pretty wicked knots."

"I just bet you do," she muttered. Did the man install an AuthorityCam to see around the corner? Stupid president, autocratic and demanding even off the job.

Grumbling, she hopped to the bathroom, found disinfectant and cotton balls, flopped onto her toilet seat, and pulled up her foot.

It was a dirty, bloody mess.

Phooey. If she hated his high-handedness, she hated worse when he was right. He was already arrogant enough.

She doused the cotton ball with disinfectant and swabbed her wounded foot, but it was like cleaning a muddy car with a makeup sponge. She just smeared the blood and dirt. So she started the water in the tub to rinse her foot instead. Then she decided she might as well shower. It was only efficient. Amazingly rational, considering she hadn't had any caffeine yet.

But in case Prince Omniscience decided to be his usual argumentative self, she locked the door.

She stripped quickly, got right in, and started shampooing. She'd worked up a good lather when the pounding started at the bathroom door.

Half-blinded, she stuck her head out. The door bowed with each thud, *Kill Door Part II*. In hindsight, locking it might not have been the smartest move. "What are you doing?"

"We need to get going." Kirk's deep voice carried easily through the composite. Another thud told her he was serious. "What are *you* doing?"

She started to yell, "I'm taking a shower," but it would only get lost in the next bang. She grabbed a towel, twisted it around her, unlocked and opened the door.

Mid-swing, Kirk's large and capable hand froze. He blinked. His gaze dropped. Widened.

Turned molten silver.

"I'm taking a shower." Her voice came out a husky whisper.

"So I see." His eyes closed and he sucked a bushel of air through distended nostrils. When he opened his eyes again they were fastened on her face. "Have you heard the weather report? No, of course not. You just woke up, didn't you?"

"Well—"

"Are you even packed?"

Her cheeks heated. "Mostly."

"Which means what, you have a suitcase out?" He blew a disgusted breath. "Don't you take anything seriously?"

"Of course I do. The important things." She straightened to her full five-three and glared. Barefoot, her glare hit mid-chest. No tie today so she had it out with the press of his pecs against a soft white sweater. His very hard, very nice pecs...she shook herself. "I care about supporting my people. About keeping up with technology. I could care less about whether we leave at eight or eight-oh-five."

His shook his head, ponytail swishing lightly. "What if five minutes makes the difference between life or death?"

"Oh, right. Because Freddy Krueger is now punching a clock."

"No, because there's a blizzard hammering Canada."

"Headed south?"

"Headed east. It's not forecast to hit us, or I wouldn't risk the drive. But I want to get an early start just in case."

Avoiding even the possibility of getting stuck in the mountains. Prudent and annoying. "Fine. I'll hurry." She slammed the bathroom door in his face.

The foot, cleaned up, wasn't nearly so bad. A couple adhesive strips took care of it. Ten minutes later she was ready to go, dressed and only slightly damp.

Kirk's gaze raked her blue jeans and sweatshirt. "You're wearing that?"

"What's wrong with casual? I like to be comfortable when I travel."

"I'm casual." He held out his arms.

Edie stared at his idea of "casual": gleaming leather loafers (were those calf?), snazzy silk socks, slim wool slacks, and cashmere sweater, all topped by a black blazer and looped scarf. "No one's going to see you except me. Why go to all that trouble?" When his expression went mulish she blew an exasperated, "Fine. Do I have time to change?"

His jaw worked briefly. "Where are your suitcases?"

She'd won—this round. She pointed to her shoulder, slung with carry-on bag, purse, and ancient laptop. Didn't want to chance her new one getting stolen. "My boots are by the door. Do I have time to make coffee?"

"We'll stop on the way." He grabbed the laptop from her as she passed. Grunted. "What's in here, a brick?"

She stopped to smile sweetly at him. "If it's too much for you…?"

"Hardly." He shrugged it onto one powerful shoulder, muscles rippling…and while she was distracted, he grabbed her carry-on. Tricky buzzard. He gave her another penetrating look. "This is awfully light. You're not wearing blue jeans to management camp, are you?"

"Relax. I have a couple lightweight suits in there." Edie started for the door. Her shoes crunched broken wood. "Nuts. I forgot about this." She brushed awed fingertips along the jamb. Sweet sex on a unicycle, it had taken enormous strength to crash through. "Why did you break my door down, anyway? Angry that I overslept?" She looked at him.

His cheeks were dark. Kirk, blushing? Impossible.

"You weren't answering," he said. "I thought you were in danger."

Edie's brows shot up. "You were *rescuing* me?"

"We can discuss it in the car. Let's go."

"Let's not." Edie headed for her landline phone. "I have to get my door fixed."

"For heaven's sake, Edie—"

"Mr. Kirk. I don't live on Snob's Hill with pricey security systems and personal guards. I have to get this door fixed."

Kirk's lips tightened. "If we get hit by snow—"

"Not going to happen. And this'll just take a minute." Edie put in a call to a neighbor who did repairs for her. While she waited for him to arrive, she breezed into the kitchen and made a pot of coffee.

*

Six hours later, Edie and Kirk were on the road. Tentatively, she said, "That wasn't too bad, was it?"

Kirk's jaw was clenched so hard, a small chin scar stood out against the white skin. "Not too bad?" His voice was exquisitely controlled and at first Edie thought she was imagining the anger radiating from him. But the teeth-grinding sound *was* rather distinctive. "Your fix-it man shows up after an hour. Then he takes off with your money, to 'get a door.' But when he returns—almost two hours later—his beer breath says he made a few other stops along the way. After all that it took him another two hours to hang a simple door." Kirk made a noise of supreme disgust. "I could have done it in half the time, for fuck's sake."

"Please don't swear. You, hang a door?" Edie tried to imagine Kirk's snow-white sweater smudged with dirt, his neat chestnut hair mussed with effort. Started to smile and mentally smacked herself. "Really?"

"Yes, me, really. But what tops it all, we took the slacker to lunch!"

"You agreed." Edie's temper flared. "You said we needed to eat anyway."

"I expected a drive-through, not slow-bake deep dish pizza."

"It's a long trip. I thought we needed a good meal before we left."

"You can't be serious. You barely ate anything."

"I found out I wasn't hungry." Should have known better than to try to eat with big bad Kirk looming next to her, radiating heat and strength and subtle cedar scent...shoot her.

"But now we're so late that, if the snowstorm veers, we're in serious trouble." His knuckles whitened on the wheel.

"The storm is stalled over Idaho. I checked the weather online before we left. When it does move, it'll head east."

"It had better." The words were dark, ominous. "Because if my car gets stuck in the mountains, it'll be thanks to you."

"That's not fair. I volunteered to take my Saab. You insisted on driving your sports sled." Although the snazzy car was comfortable. And the engine's deep thrum was very sexy.

"My 'sled' has all-wheel drive."

"Whatever. Point is, if there's a storm and if we get caught in it, two very big 'ifs', we'd have stood a far better chance in my car. It's bigger and heavier."

Everett raised a brow at her. "The wonderful classic Saab put in storage by your uncle Jake before he moved to the ashram in India? How old is it, again?"

"It's in excellent condition." She flushed, wishing she'd never babbled those details. But she'd had to fill the time waiting for the door *some*how. "Front-wheel drive and great snow tires—"

"And *ancient*. My sports car is less than a year old."

"With barely enough room in the trunk for a handkerchief."

"A bit of an exaggeration, since we got all our luggage in there—"

"We had to stuff the laptops behind the seats."

"May I finish a sentence?"

"If it's short."

His lips quirked, like a suppressed smile. "We managed to fit everything."

Darn him for being reasonable. "I hate it when you're right."

The smile broke free, his dimple slaying her. "Thank you. Edie, my car has modern safety equipment. It's far safer than yours."

He had an answer for everything, naturally. She crossed her arms and stared out the window. "What about Project Pleiades? That's due next Friday, and without me around to manage it...oh no. You didn't give it to *her*, did you?"

"I wouldn't do that to you. Jack will head it in your absence. Bethany will only get involved if he has questions." He paused. "I got the original deadline reinstated."

"Wow. That's good. Thanks." How had he managed that miracle? Better not ask. He'd probably done something super heroic and it would only go to his head.

Miles passed in comfortable silence. But when a couple flakes of snow hit the windshield, Kirk's knuckles whitened again. Then the sky turned leaden with sullen pregnant clouds. Kirk's jaw tightened. He didn't say anything but his tension screamed *your fault.*

Or maybe she just had a guilty conscience.

But she didn't see how she could've done things differently. She replayed the morning in her mind. It wasn't her fault she needed to replace her door. Not her fault he refused her car.

She was *not* at fault. And even if she was, a teeny-tiny bit, Kirk should have apologized for his part in it, breaking the door. But no. Company presidents blamed the help.

Whatever had possessed him to break down her door anyway? Come to think of it, what had possessed him to insist on driving her today? They did nothing but argue. She wasn't on Everett Kirk's bucket list, yet he'd saddled himself with her for four days total. Inexplicable, inconceivable.

Maybe he was going to lecture her. She was confined. Aside from sticking her fingers in her ears and singing the verses she wasn't supposed to know from *Barnacle Bill*, she couldn't stop him. The signs of civilization slipped away. She eyed Everett surreptitiously. Maybe he wasn't just going to lecture her. Maybe he meant to teach her a lesson physically. He was a foot taller and probably outweighed her by fifty pounds plus, so she couldn't stop him if he decided she needed a lesson in obedience...ooh, obedience. Bad girl. And Kirk in black leather and studs ...well, he *did* know those wicked knots...her eyes flew open. For shizzle's sake, he was her *boss*. Kinky sex with Kirk was like deep-fried pizza, just wrong. Hot and juicy and oh-so tasty...but wrong.

Mile after silent mile passed, not nearly so comfortable now. Traffic thinned under angry clouds spitting flurries. Soon Kirk's car seemed to be the only one on the road. Even road signs were few and far between. As night approached, Edie shifted in her seat. The scattered snow didn't bother her; Kirk's intentions did. Her nerves frayed more with each passing mile. After an hour, she was concerned enough to broach the uncomfortable silence. "Um, so what are your driving plans?"

He glanced at her, his eyes silver mirrors hiding his thoughts, his intentions. "I-70 to Highway 15."

"No, I mean stops. Where are we eating dinner? Where are we—spending the night?"

Silver flicked back to the road. "Don't worry. It's going on the company credit card."

"That wasn't what was bothering me."

He cut her a startled look. "Edie, I'm a professional. You don't have to worry that I'll do anything untoward."

She relaxed, immensely relieved that he didn't intent to paddle her or worse...or better...his reply registered. He'd thought she'd meant... "Oh, that wasn't it either!" Mostly.

"Glad to hear it," he said dryly. "We have two room reservations in Cedar City. We should get there around ten thirty, if there are no delays." He paused. "As a fall back, I have a summer place in the mountains."

"Good." *Not*. Alone in a mountain hideaway, with Everett Kirk and his wicked knots? Even if he were totally professional, what if she overslept again? Would he break down her bedroom door? Scoop her up effortlessly and dump her in the shower? Kirk's big hand, peeling back her robe as he blasted her with the shower, his eyes molten silver as when they coursed down her near-naked body—

Not oversleeping. "Uh, I think I'll take a little nap."

Everett nodded. "Glad you trust me. I'll wake you when we get there."

"Great." Edie closed her eyes. Finding surprisingly that she did trust him, she drifted off to sleep.

*

She dreamed. The flurries and her insane hours at HHE got mixed up with working late at her first job at Broad Vistas Computer Consultants, and getting stranded in the snow.

January. Working hard, newbie Edie never registered the blizzard scale goes from flurries to oh crap. At 7 p.m. she packed up and exited the building.

And stood, astonished at the blanched empty parking lot. Behind her, the security door clicked shut.

She spun, knowing she'd pulled a Homer; she hadn't gotten her keycard yet and couldn't get back in. She patted mittened hands against the glass, tugged ineffectively at the locked door.

Panic's infinite loop broke when she remembered she had a car, borrowed from her roommate until she could afford her own. She trotted eagerly to where she'd left it.

Snow and sleet whipped across the desolate asphalt, skittering noisily like a plague of tap dancing locusts. Only one other vehicle was in the lot, a pickup truck crusted with white. She had no idea if someone was still in the building or if the owner had simply bailed.

Her borrowed car was an old rear-wheel-drive hatch that her roommate called "vintage" and Edie called "wreckage." She fumbled the key into the lock, clumsy in mittens and shivers. When the door finally opened, she fell into the car, tripped by a gust. Shutting the door barely muffled the wind's scream.

A push of gas, a turn of key, a heartfelt prayer, and sweat-strewn moments later she was rewarded with a deep-throated *vroom*. Saved! The worst was over. She put the car in gear and fed gas.

And promptly spun out. The lot was an ice rink. Her boots' tread had kept her from skating, but bald tires had as much grip as skis. It took all her driving expertise to get the thing sliding in a straight line toward the exit.

Which was uphill.

The incline wasn't steep, but ice made it slick. Like a cat running on a freshly waxed floor, the car slipped sideways. After several tries she stopped, temporarily beaten.

By now she was panting, tiny white puffs of air. She took inventory. Cell phone, out of juice, no car charger. Some cash, but as a newbie she didn't know what, if any, stores were within walking distance or if they were even open. Maybe something helpful was in the trunk. She started to turn off the engine.

No, it had taken three miracles and a beatification to start it. Leaving it running, she popped the trunk and got out. Her roommate's emergency supplies were a cracked shovel and a torn bag of cat litter draining into the spare tire well.

Sure, the worst was over. The Great God of Gotcha was laughing his butt off. She dragged out the litter. By sprinkling some under the rear tires, inching forward, stopping and sprinkling more litter on the new patch, she was able to climb a good three feet up the slope in a half an hour.

She was almost to the top when the car ran out of gas.

"Da...gnation. Shi...zzle. Fu...zznuck." She bonked her forehead on the steering wheel. She would have loved to vent with a good thick curse but her grandparents taught her swearing was verbal laziness and Rowans were never lazy.

Something moved in her periphery. She jerked upright—Broad Vistas's door had opened. She leaped out of the car with a shout. A gust of wind stole her cry. Snow blasted her eyes. By the time her vision cleared the door was shut.

An eerie silence descended. Edie choked on a sob. Had she imagined the door opening?

The roar of a powerful vehicle jumpstarted her heart. The veil of snow parted, revealing a riced-up 4x4.

The truck ate its way to her side. The driver's fogged window rolled down, revealing a silver-haired man with intelligent brown eyes magnified by gold-rimmed glasses. "Need some help?"

That was how Edie met her mentor, Philip Sedgwick.

Chapter Three

To: ThePrez@serenityrangers.com
From: ED@mythicmail.com
Subject: Re: About me

Dear Ev E.E. Hardass,

You're punny. A man (or woman) after my own heart. I like E.E. My college friends call me E.E. too. But I've gotten to think of you as Prez so I guess I'll stick with that.

You're definitely not a Hardass. You brighten my day too, and I always look forward to your emails. Those jerks at your office do not appreciate the funny, wonderful person you are.

Remember, if cars were computers, twice a day, for no reason at all, they'd crash.

—ED

Edie woke halfway when Kirk stopped at a rest area. She cast a bleary eye at the clock. Two hours had passed.

He opened her door. Chilly air spilled in, waking her fast. They must be well into Utah by now. His hand lifted her out. She looked around. The grass was covered with snow but the air and the walkway were clear, so she didn't think anything of it. After a five-minute break, they were on the road again.

By now the sky was black, the kind that comes from laden clouds at night.

Kirk drove with intense focus. Edie wasn't sure why until she saw big white flakes smack into the window.

"It's snowing," she said.

He raised both brows. "I'm amazed at your powers of observation."

"I'm amazed at your powers of sarcasm, Kirk."

"*Mr.* Kirk."

"Then call me Ms. Rowan."

"That's not company policy."

"It's Saturday. We're not on company time."

"This is a company function."

"You always have an answer, don't you?" Worry made her sharp. She crossed her arms and glared at him. It bounced off his rock-hard profile. "Okay, if this is work, I get overtime."

Muscles in his jaw bunched. "Can we drop this for now? I have enough to deal with."

He had a point. The snow was coming fast and heavy, like driving into a kaleidoscope of long white needles. "What happened?"

"The impossible. The storm hooked south. It's been doing this off and on for the last hour."

"The Great Gotcha laughs again."

"What?"

"Nothing. What do we do?"

"Go to Plan B." He exited north onto a two-lane crowned road, the kind humped high in the middle for drainage, with ditches on either side.

"Your summer place?" The mountain hideaway, alone with him and his wicked knots? Edie's anxiety notched up. "How far?"

"About fifteen minutes, I think."

"You think? You're not sure?"

"It's a recent purchase, and the signs are covered over with snow. But it's two rights and a left. I'm sure."

"You're *sure.*"

"Try to hold down the sarcasm, please. It's frosting the windows."

She waited but the window stayed frosted and the snow got worse. "Maybe we should ask for directions."

"Nobody around to ask. Anyway, it's not necessary. I know where we are."

"You think."

"I know." A pause. "I'm virtually certain."

"Is that like virtual reality? How about we turn around and find somewhere more populated to wait out the storm. Okay, Kirk?"

"My summer house is no more than fifteen minutes away. And it's Mr. Kirk."

"Yes sir, Mr. Kirk sir."

He glared at her—and suddenly they were slipping sideways.

"Everett!" Edie grabbed the seat, hard.

"I've got it." His strong hands, gripping the wheel, eased the car out of its skid.

She released the seat after a moment. "Nicely done." She strained to see past the veil of white. "When was the last sign of civilization?"

"Edie, we'll be at my house in fifteen minutes. Don't worry."

"I'm not worried."

"Of course not." His voice was gentle. "Why don't you harangue me about employee rights?"

"Somehow, Kirk, I don't feel like it right now." She peered into the driving snow, bracing herself for the next horrible skid.

"Edie, if you could see your way clear to using *Mr.* Kirk—"

"The whole point is I can't see clearly, and it's been at least fifteen minutes, Mr. Edward Everett Kirk." She couldn't help the edge to her voice, more anxiety than heat. "Shouldn't we have been there by now?"

"We're traveling much slower than I anticipated. It threw off my sense of timing. But it can't be much farther."

Her eyes hurt from squinting into the driving white. Nothing, no houses, no signs, nothing but trees. She couldn't even see the mountain peaks. Until...

For an instant the swirling snow parted. She glimpsed a log cabin.

"Everett, stop!"

He hit the brakes. The whole car shuddered as the anti-lock brake system kicked in. "What's wrong?"

"There's a cabin back there, near the road."

"Not mine. Mine isn't near the road." He started the car forward.

"Can't we pull off, maybe wait out the storm?"

"You see how the snow is piling up. Our best bet is to continue to my summer house."

"But Everett," Edie began, just as the car began to slide.

With remarkable calm, Everett steered into the skid. The road was narrow, no shoulder and no margin for error, but he was good. Correcting with competent hands and clenched jaw he managed to get them almost straightened out.

A huge gust of wind hit them broadside. The light sports car, caught too near the edge, was pushed off the sloped road.

The car slid, spinning slightly, for what seemed like an eternity, soundless but for the rasping of Edie's breath. Then it ground to a halt nose first in a mountain of white.

*

Time snapped forward. The sudden stop was enough to jar Edie but not enough to trigger the airbags. They'd plowed into deeper snow, not really a mountain, but getting back on the road wasn't an option.

Still, she had to hand it to Kirk—he tried. He put the car in reverse and tried to power out. He put the car in gear and tried to power out. He tried rocking between reverse and first. But the snow was too deep. Even cat litter in the trunk wouldn't have helped—though she rather doubted Kirk would dirty his expensive sports car with a bag of common clay.

"Don't worry," he said. "I have satellite navigation. We can locate my house and hike there when there's a break in the storm."

Edie gaped at him. "You've had GPS this whole time and you haven't bothered to turn it on?" Philip Sedgwick would never have waited until now to mention the GPS. Of course, Philip would never have gotten them into this mess in the first place. He had a truck, big and seriously kitted out—although not to the point that it screamed compensation. Much.

"I didn't need directions. The house is nearby. Now we'll find out how close." Calmly, Kirk keyed the GPS on.

Nothing happened.

"What's wrong?" Besides being stranded in the snow with no idea of where they were, no silver-haired mentor hovered conveniently nearby.

"The system appears to be broken. Maybe it never worked." He shrugged. "I haven't ever used it."

Of course he hadn't. "You're such a guy."

He raised a brow. "You say that like it's an insult."

"No. If I called you an executive, that'd be an insult."

"Well, thank goodness for your restraint. We're not out of options yet." Kirk extracted a slim phone from his breast pocket and thumbed 911. Frowned. "Damn."

"Please don't swear. What's the matter?"

"No signal."

Edie tried her own phone with the same results. "Okay then. If high-tech solutions don't work, go low-tech." She zipped her jacket and popped the door. Snow pelted her as she scrabbled out.

"What are you doing?" Kirk grabbed her jacket and hauled her back in.

She landed half-sprawled on the seat. "Hey." She pushed his hand off, trying not to notice how big and capable it was. "I'm hiking to that cabin I saw. It won't take long."

"Oh no you don't. You'll get lost."

"Says Mr. Two Rights and a Left."

"Point. All right, but I'll come with you."

Point? He'd acknowledged she was right? She hid her surprise. "In those shoes?"

He glanced down at his loafers. "You're wearing running shoes."

"I have boots in the trunk."

"Right again. Good for you." Exasperation and amusement laced his tone. "I'm still coming with you."

"Suit yourself." She scrambled out of the car, then grabbed her purse from the seat well and slung it across her chest. Big wet flakes splattered all over her. "Hope your snappy outfit's washable."

"Smug is not your style," he called out after her.

She smiled, though it was lost in the howling white. When he wasn't doing his it's-good-to-be-king thing he was pretty cute... oh, not thinking that.

He popped the trunk. As she pulled out her boots he joined her, adjusting the computers over his shoulders.

She exchanged footwear and zipped up. "I think it's being on the other end of smug that's not your style, Kirk."

"Company time, Edie. Mr. Kirk, please. Are you certain there's a cabin back there?" He was standing so close she could feel the steam rise off his rapidly dampening body.

"Yes." She shivered, blamed it on the cold. "If I didn't know better I'd think you were insisting on the 'mister' to distract me from being worried."

"Would I do that?" He frowned at the car, embedded in white. "That's not going anywhere. Let's take our luggage. Anyway, if you insist on being familiar, I'd prefer Everett to Kirk."

"You believe that I saw a cabin?" she asked. He trusted her?

He looked at her in surprise. "Of course. Why would you lie about it?"

Of course. Why would she? It was her frozen butt on the line too.

He pulled out his suitcases and her bag, slammed the trunk shut and slogged off. Cases and bag in hand, double-slung with computer bags, he looked like a luggage rack (albeit a strong, lithe one). She was amazed he could even move, festooned with cases like that. Yet he tramped through the snow briskly, surprisingly sure-footed. Maybe she'd underestimated him.

Nah, probably just couldn't conceive mere snow would dare trip a man of his importance. Like nature cared about pay grade. He'd slip and fall, breaking a dozen or so bones.

Which would be a crying shame, marring that strong, lithe body... lock her in *Warehouse 13*. His falling would be bad because they were stranded and she'd be the one who'd have to care for him. She ran after him and grabbed her bag and laptop. With her boots and lighter weight, she quickly took the lead, Kirk lumbering behind her. "Say, are those designer suitcases?" she shouted back.

"Could you enjoy this a bit less obviously?"

She grinned, knowing he wouldn't see it but betting he could feel it. "Feet frozen yet?"

"I'm moving. Can't get frostbite while moving. Damn!" A man-sized thud preempted the howling wind.

Her stomach dropped. She spun. He'd fallen to his knees. She started to run back to him.

He surged to his feet, easily, without even releasing his hold on the cases. "How far to that cabin?"

She stopped, blinking. The man had hidden strength. "Not much farther. I could carry your computer."

His hot glare cut through the snow. "I can manage my own luggage, thank you."

"Right." Striking out again, she nearly missed the dark blur of the cabin she'd seen from the road. "This way."

"I don't see anything. I hope you know where you're—"

"Here it is." She traipsed up three stairs to the porch, too relieved to give him the smugness he deserved. She set down her bag and tried the knob. "Batter-fried phooey. It's locked."

He set his luggage next to hers. "I'll take care of it."

"Not on your life. We need this door to protect us from the snow and wind."

"I don't habitually break down doors." Kirk dug around in his computer case, eventually producing what looked like the illegitimate offspring of a Swiss Army knife and a mad dentist.

"What's that?"

"Nothing." He pulled a slim rod from the back of the knife, selected one of the probe tools, bent to the keyhole, and jiggered it. Within minutes, a snap cut through the wind. Kirk pushed the door open. "After you."

"Now who's being smug? Where'd you get the lock picks?" Crossing the threshold, Edie plunged into darkness.

"A misspent youth. Is it warm?"

"Deliciously toasty." She set down her computer and hunted for a light switch. The empty cabin was actually quite cold, but at least she was out of the wind. Her fingers stuttered over a row of hanger-wire coat hooks, finally landing on a heavy plastic switch. She flipped it and breathed thanks when yellow light flooded the room.

Kirk dragged in the rest of the luggage and shut the door. The howling sliced off. "First things first. Heat." His smooth baritone dropped loudly into the silence left by the wind.

"And a phone?"

"Why don't you look for that while I bump the thermostat up from icicle?"

"Okay." They were in a single great room, one side decorated as a living room, the other as a kitchen. In back, a narrow hallway indicated more cabin. Two facing doors and a curtained opening were hopefully comfortable bedrooms and a bathroom.

Edie felt herself relaxing. The cabin reminded her of vacationing as a girl with her grandparents. Maybe this wouldn't be so bad. It might even be nice. Maybe Kirk could also relax in this remote, intimate setting. Maybe a reasonable man lurked under that corporate mask. Her eyes automatically sought him out.

Kirk prowled the room like a loose-limbed lion, hunting the elusive thermostat. Escaped strands of chestnut hair framed his strong cheeks. Expensive wet clothes clung to a large, well-shaped frame. He'd tossed the scarf, revealing a muscular throat.

She shook herself. Phone, phone… An old-fashioned landline cable threaded the back wall. She traced it to a chunky phone atop a stack of milk crates.

"Ah. Here it is." He was examining a simple dial-style thermostat. She was distracted a moment by his capable hands resetting it.

A furnace kicked in. He grinned at her, the boyish pride shining on his face sending a jolt to her gut. He said, "Oh, you found the phone. Great. Call the office. I'll have them send us a helicopter. We'll be out of here in no time."

Edie's fingers convulsed on the handset. He couldn't stand the idea of being stuck with her a moment longer than he absolutely had to.

Well, what did she expect, with all the bickering they did? Did she really think that he'd see this place as a haven too? That he'd relax, toss the corporate manners along with the scarf? "It's Saturday night. Who'll be there?"

"My secretary."

"Figures," Edie said under her breath. Fine, get it over with. She put the handset to her ear and—no dial tone. She frowned at Kirk. "It's off."

He strode across the room, grabbed the phone from her and listened intently. "You're right."

"I'm too technologically challenged to know a disconnected phone when I hear one?" Edie stripped off her wet jacket.

"Of course not. Don't be so touchy." He cradled the handset. "It's possible the phone isn't disconnected, but that the line is down."

"So? Out of order is out of order."

"After the storm's over, a broken line will be repaired. If it is, I can call Ms. Dooley."

Of course he could. "It's Saturday night. Tomorrow's Sunday, for schnitzel's sake. However long it takes, your faithful secretary will be there to answer?" *Woof,* she thought.

"She forwards calls to her cell on weekends. Since we're going to be here a while, why don't you see if there's food? I'm going to check the back." He strode into the hallway.

"Get out of those wet clothes first." Edie hung her jacket on a wall hook. The sound of spitting air came from the back of the cabin. Lucking fovely, there was another thing she'd have to fix, after finding food. Certainly citizen Pentus Houseus Kirkus would be no help coping with anything rustic. Although he had worker's hands. She liked his hands. "At least hang up your coat to dry."

"Not yet." He emerged from the curtained opening. "I need to go back outside."

"Why?"

"The water pump is off. And the utility line for the furnace comes in behind that curtain. According to the gauge, we're almost out of oil."

Edie's cheeks tingled with vestiges of cold. "We'll freeze."

"In a mountain full of trees? I don't think so." Kirk pointed to the living room, where a comfortable potbellied stove stood in the corner.

She perked up instantly. "There's a pile of logs outside. I'll get some."

"Those logs need to be cut and split, useless unless we find an ax. I saw some dead trees. There'll be brush and broken branches we can use."

"But you're wet. You'll catch cold." She felt the strangest urge to protect him.

"Exactly. I'm wet already. I won't get wetter."

"But I have boots."

"Edie." He clasped her shoulders, the heat from his hands fiery in the still-cool room. "Learn to delegate."

For once, Edie couldn't think of a thing to say. She let him walk out, the imprint of his hands burning her shoulders.

Chapter Four

To: ED@mythicmail.com
From: ThePrez@serenityrangers.com
Subject: Re: Re: About me

Ha! I'm a wonderful person :) You said it and you can't take it back. My self-worth is restored.

And you're an E.E. like me! I think you must have a balanced head on your shoulders.

Can I ask you a question? A serious question, about a problem at work.

—Prez

Scratching up wood and searching for the well gave Everett too much time to think.

Being stranded wasn't going to do his career any favors. Bad enough he was out of the office for a week and couldn't counter the nasty rumors in person. He'd counted on his smartphone, computer, and Ms. Dooley to head off any power plays. Now his faithful secretary stood alone. She was an outstanding assistant but no bastion to weather the deadly storm of corporate infighting.

Too bad it wasn't Edie standing for him in Denver. She was bastion and offensive battalion all rolled into one.

If Edie were on his side. His mind started down a darker path.

She'd taken getting stranded rather well. Almost happy when the phone didn't work. Even more damning, she'd delayed them so long that their stranding seemed almost inevitable.

Was it planned?

Someone was trying to drive him out of HHE. He'd thought it was Howell Junior.

But now Everett wondered.

It made uncomfortable sense. She was the company's best manager. But he worked half his week just trying to keep her out of trouble. She fought him constantly, opposing his decisions and even his right to make them where the employees were concerned. She always seemed to inject her personal brand of mayhem just when it would damage him the most.

Coincidence? Or did her unerring sense of timing display a deeper knowledge of the squabbling and infighting of HHE and its ultra-conservative board?

Then Everett laughed. Edie, a corporate shark? No way. She was too honest, her face too open, for her to deceive him that way. Besides, the Edie he knew would never kill a man's career with suspicion and innuendo.

So who? Everett dropped a load of brush near the cabin and ran a hand through his semi-frozen hair. The latest abuse had happened just this morning.

Everett was getting ready to pick up Edie, trying to decide between a silk set that was snappy and a wool set that was smart. Neither was terribly comfortable, but for some reason he'd wanted to impress her.

Ms. Dooley called. "Problem, Mr. Kirk. The board is not pleased with the state of the finances."

"Why? The preliminary fourth quarter figures show a profit."

"The revised reports posted on the company intranet show a loss."

"*What?* Where did those come from?"

"I don't know, sir. I'm only repeating what Mr. Howell said. The son, not the father."

Junior. There was a prime candidate for Everett's unknown tormentor. When Howell Senior handed Everett the presidency, Junior had stalked out and never forgiven either of them.

Everett stomped his frozen feet, wincing at a sick crackling sound. Hopefully not his toes. Time to stop worrying about corporate survival and concentrate on physical survival. Edie was counting on him. That was enough wood. The well next. Although they could always drink melted snow, he'd rather be able to flush the toilet. He located the well under the roof of what appeared to be a chicken house and activated the pump.

Then he trudged back to the cabin and picked up a load of wood, crackling the whole way. Not his toes, his shoes. Five hundred dollars of Italian leather down the drain.

Crap.

Then he thought of Edie's short red curls dusted with snow, her cheeks flushed from the cold, her eyes bright. Waiting for him inside.

Maybe things weren't so bad, after all.

*

"You're melting all over that wood, Kirk. It'll never burn that way. Don't you know anything about fires?" Edie pulled the brush out of Kirk's dripping arms. She was yelling at him about the wood because shrieking, "You've been gone too long!" would sound like maybe she'd been worried about him. Which she *hadn't*. Though he'd had the nerve to stagger in, face pinched and body half ice like a Kirkcicle. Was the man *trying* to get sick?

"Being wet is not by choice, Edie. And it's Everett, remember?"

"Right." Thought she believed in equality between staff and management, calling Mr. President Kirk by his first name seemed so...intimate. "I checked the cabin for supplies while you were gone." Way too long. Not shrieking. "Little food. No water. And..." Talk about intimate. "Only one bedroom."

"We'll have water in a bit. I found a well and switched on the pump."

"Good. Thanks." She was surprised, assuming she'd be the expert during this little crisis. Maybe he'd be useful after all.

"You're welcome. We'll have heat from the wood burner, so let's save the oil." Everett spun off the thermostat while Edie stuffed wood into the stove. "All right, let's see how good that pump is." In the kitchen, he twisted on the tap. Air and water spat in equal measure. "Should have primed it, damn it."

"Please don't swear." She picked up the long lighter from on top of the stove, clicked it on and stuck it into the depths of the wood.

"Why? What's wrong with swearing?"

The wood refused to light. "My grandparents taught me swearing is a crutch for the verbally unimaginative. Stupid wet wood." She looked up. "Speaking of, you should change."

"Soon. That's not how you stack wood." He stopped playing with the sink to come and kneel next to her.

A pleasant scent enveloped her, cedar and pine and warm male. The lighter trembled in her hand. She released the trigger. "Change, Kirk. You must have something dry in that trousseau of yours."

"Brides have trousseaux. I have luggage. And it's Everett. Here, let me." He grabbed a branch and yanked it out of the stove. Wood tumbled onto the floor.

Edie sprang to her feet, pleasant scent driven from her mind. "Now see what you've done."

"It's okay. You had too much packed in there. Start a fire small."

"I've made fires before." Camp and bonfires, but wood was wood.

He started diligently snapping off twigs and peeling bark. "Did you check that the flue was open? That's that lever there."

She scowled, pulled it. The pipe shuddered with a sharp *kawang*. "Kirk, I was making the fire fine."

"Everett." He stuck his head into the stove. "And you were doing it wrong."

"Why are you always telling me I'm wrong?" She smacked the stove. It rang satisfyingly around his head.

"Ouch." He pulled abruptly out. "I'm not always telling you you're wrong."

"See, you just did it again. You're telling me I'm wrong that you're always telling me I'm wrong."

Everett pinched the bridge of his nose. "Why are you always questioning my abilities?"

"I'm not questioning your abilities. I'm questioning your authority."

"All right, I'll bite." His eyes gleamed almost silver in soot-dusted skin. His voice was annoyingly level. "Why do you question my authority?"

"Because being company president doesn't automatically make you an authority on everything. You're not VP of Wood Burning Stoves. An MBA from UCLA doesn't make you..."

"Edie, my MBA's from Harvard. Are we having the same discussion?"

"I meant Harvard." Edie turned away. Had she been arguing with President Everett about making a fire—or with VP Philip over a pregnant woman?

*

From the day Philip Sedgwick rescued Edie, he was her hero. He, in turn, patiently tutored her in all aspects of humane management. She idolized him, lifting him to just one notch below her beloved grandparents.

And then he sucker-punched her. All over Aurora Thode.

Aurora wasn't part of Edie's team, but she was a colleague, a fellow programmer. Another little guy. No one knew Aurora was sleeping with the boss until her third trimester.

Then it was rather obvious.

Rumors flew about the father's identity, possibilities ranging from the comptroller to the CEO. The one thing the rumors agreed on was that the father was an executive, and that he'd refused to marry Aurora. Edie didn't listen to rumors, but she couldn't help hearing Aurora shouting in the shuttered conference room, or the low patronizing voice answering. Edie couldn't make out words until Aurora unleashed her ultimatum. "You'd better marry me or I'll reveal your identity to the whole company!"

She got fired instead.

Everybody went about their business afterward like nothing happened, except they were hushed and their eyes were wide.

Except Edie. She marched righteously into the company president's office. "Employees have rights!" Mentally, her grandparents were cheering.

The president, Martin Leaderman, was a silver corporatosaur. Philip called him "Leadbottom" behind his back.

Leaderman sat behind a gargantuan cherrywood desk in the middle of a cavernous office. His ergonomic calfskin chair cost more than Edie's secondhand car.

"It's none of your business, Ms. Rowan." Leaderman didn't even bother looking up from his paperwork.

Edie crossed the room in three angry strides and slapped her hand over his papers. "What you did to Aurora is inexcusable. I'll report it."

"Oh?" Leaderman's cold eyes finally rose to meet hers. "To whom?"

That stopped her. She'd only thought in terms of confronting Leaderman, not what she'd do if he refused to listen. Who could she report this to? A good trial lawyer. And the Department of Labor…maybe even the Supreme Court. But first, especially, Philip. "Everyone I can. You're in trouble now, Leadbottom."

"What did you call me?" Leaderman suffused an angry red. "Get the hell out."

Edie stalked out. With Philip Sedgwick to support her, she'd right this injustice.

But Philip *laughed* at her.

"You're an ass, Edie. Calling him Leadbottom to his face? Dumber than a bag of hammers."

She chewed her lip. "But you call him that."

"Not where he can hear me, you fucking idiot."

Words failed her. Philip always praised her. He was her mentor, her idol. Now she felt two years old. Finally she stuttered, "But what about Aurora? She's due soon and won't have health insurance."

In a cold tone she'd never forget, Philip said, "It was her own damn fault. Stupid bitch."

"Edie?" Everett's deep voice cut through her thoughts. "Edie, I wasn't trying to insult your abilities. But I did a stint in Serenity Rangers International and learned some survival tricks overseas. Watching you stuff that wood in like cartoon dynamite was giving me a headache. So could I build the fire—please?"

Please? Edward Everett Kirk, president and CEO, had said please? She rubbed her eyes and turned.

He stood there in his sodden, expensive clothes that were curiously comic, his silver-blue eyes curiously kind, the tiny scar on his chin making him curiously vulnerable.

She waved in the direction of the stove. "All right."

He unleashed the killer dimple. While she reeled, he stacked kindling and lit it. Within minutes he had a crackling fire in the stove, feeding bigger pieces in until heat poured into the room.

Edie did not tell him she was impressed.

*

"And now I'm going to get out of this wet clothing." Everett disappeared into the back hallway.

Finally. "Good."

He returned with a bucket. "And take a bath."

Edie stared at him. "Are you nuts? Everett, you may be able to build fires, but you have no concept of roughing it. We don't even have running water yet." To show him how overly optimistic he was being, she turned on the kitchen tap. Spitting air combined with a thin trickle. She stuck a finger in. "Brr. Even the air coming out is cold. The water's liquid ice."

"No problem." He opened the front door.

"You think you'll find water littering the ground outside?"

Everett turned, one of his fine chestnut eyebrows raised. "You're kidding, right?" Cashmere clinging damply to his big frame, he let himself out.

"The man's insane," Edie muttered. "His brain froze and cracked in half."

The door whacked open and Everett trudged in with a bucket of snow. She followed him to the bathroom. "Kirk, stop. Think. You're pneumonia waiting to happen and yet you're taking a snow bath?"

"It's Everett." He dumped snow into the tub. "You could boil some snow into hot water." He dazzled her with a hopeful smile, and strode back out.

"He's swinging on his logic gates." She found a couple pots and when he dragged in another bucket semaphored them at him: s-t-o-p. Apparently he didn't read semaphore because he swept by her. Or maybe it was her accent. "At least change into dry clothes to go outside." She trotted after him.

"They'll just get wet too." He dumped the snow into the tub.

"Everett, please."

"Aw. You said Everett." He grinned, hitting her full-on with the dimple, and then escaped while she flailed like a stupid deer.

"Grr." She dug out two pots of snow, slapped them onto the stove. The door opened. She spun, determined to stop him.

He smiled as he came through, dimple set on stun.

She raised sarcasm shields. "My dream bath. A mountain of snow dissolved in a few cups of hot water."

He reemerged from the bathroom, sans bucket and wrestling off his wet coat. "It'll be fine. Better stir those. You can actually scorch water, you know."

"For skit's sake. We're lost in the mountains with no phone, you're about to freeze your ask off, and you're lecturing me on burnt water?" She waited while he hung the coat on a hook. But when he went back into the bathroom without responding, she trotted after him. "Don't do this, please. You'll catch your death! Everett, are you listening?"

"I always listen. I just don't always agree. All this hauling is actually making me quite hot."

"That's not—"

He stripped the sweater over his head. It revealed a wet tee molded to his muscled chest.

Her eyes widened. Her mouth stayed open. No more words emerged.

Under his conservative cover, Everett Kirk had savage Tarzan's torso. Heavy pectorals stood out over a washboard belly, swept into brawny arms sparking with short golden hair. Bulges slid intriguingly as he tossed the cashmere over the sink.

Edie snapped her mouth shut. She was not impressed. Not at all. She snatched up the sweater. "This needs to be blocked. Do you want it to pull out of shape?"

"No." Unbuckling his belt, he smiled. "Thanks."

She pressed a hand to her breastbone, her heart hammering underneath. This wasn't fair. Pampered executives did not look like this. They were pale and doughy, or glowing with a cancerous tan and muscles courtesy of a toning class. Those powerful muscles said Everett worked for his physique, invested time and sweat in something other than money. He might be more than just a corporate shark.

She heated dangerously at the thought.

He stripped off the belt.

Wrong, wrong, *wrong*. Just because he was nice to her occasionally, and could make a fire, just because he could say please and had a lovely smile and stunning chest...and below...

He was unzipping.

With a squeak, she fled.

Chapter Five

To: ThePrez@serenityrangers.com
From: ED@mythicmail.com
Subject: Last message

You can ask me a serious question if you want—believe me, I know about the sinkhole called office politics. Sometimes just venting about your problem helps. I'll listen. What are friends for?
—ED

After insulting Leadbottom, Edie joined Aurora Thode on the unemployment line. Months went by before she finally found a job. Desperate, she accepted a low-paying position at a sweatshop that cared nothing for her as an employee and even less for her as a person. She almost lost her idealism then, almost submitted to crawling despair. Then she'd gotten the phone call.

"Edie, it's Philip Sedgwick. I know you're still upset, but please listen."

"What do you want, Philip?"

"I have a new job, my dear. Vice president of finance for Houghton Howell Enterprises."

"Congratulations. And I should care, why?"

"They're looking for programmers. Interested?"

She pretended not to be. "I'm a team leader where I am."

"Even better. HHE is team-based, and there's an opening. Remember our discussions on management philosophy? I bet you'd be super."

"Is it a sweatshop?"

"Not with me here, my dear."

Edie was working for HHE within a month. She forgave Philip, but she never quite trusted him the way she had.

*

Everett scrubbed clean in record time and dried himself so briskly he almost singed his body hair. Which, considering he was a mass of goose bumps, would've been an improvement. Still, once he was dry and wrapped in his kimono-style robe he was comfortable. The woodstove heated the cabin nicely.

He emerged from the bathroom cautiously. Edie was prowling around the cabin, shooting little glances at him, pretending she didn't want to argue. He found it…cute. Not safe to find a tiny tigress of a woman cute, but there it was. He flopped down in the single living room chair, kicked his bare feet onto the coffee table, picked up a magazine and casually flipped through it. That should get her started.

"Did you enjoy your bath?"

"Immensely," he lied. He flipped another page. "You said you'd found food?"

"A little." She glanced at the cabinets, the thin line of her mouth telling him more than her words. "Let me know when you're hungry and I'll see what I can do with it."

Over the pages of his magazine, Everett watched her. It was obvious to him that she was starving, but this was Edie. No way she would let herself appear vulnerable.

He closed the magazine and rose. "I'm hungry. Show me what you found."

Fifteen minutes later, a disappointingly small assortment of non-perishables lay on the table. He picked up a can and frowned at it. "Peaches." He set it down and rattled a wire-tied bag. "Brown rice."

She rolled a cardboard canister in her hands. "Oatmeal. A little of this and a little of that."

"And not much of anything." He grunted. "Want some dry cereal?"

An odd gleam lit her eyes. "Since you made the fire, why don't I try my hand at dinner?"

"The little woman cooks? Won't that offend your ideas of equality?"

"Really, Everett, must you be so disagreeable? It's called sharing the workload. Go back to your magazine." Her eyes fluttered down to his chest. The gleam intensified.

His groin tightened. She'd looked that way at him when he'd stripped off the sweater. It gave him hope. He looked down at himself. His kimono had worked loose, the neck gaping to his abdomen.

And she was interested in what she saw. He felt a smile bloom on his face.

She looked away. She was blushing.

He tucked his robe closed, smile broadening. She tried so hard to be invulnerable, but her redhead's complexion gave her away every time. "Okay. But let me know if you need me." *Need me.* He was gratified to see her blush deepen. Smiling to himself, he returned to the chair and picked up the business weekly, but he didn't read it. Instead, he watched her.

Her color returned to normal. She seemed oblivious to him, humming softly to herself as she picked up things on the table, set them down, drummed her fingers, then picked them up again. Evidently reaching a decision, she twisted the electric oven on and started dragging out pots and pans.

The whys and wherefores of what she was doing were opaque to him, but Everett certainly admired how she dragged out those pots and pans. The way her slim backside wiggled as she tried to reach something in the back…he quickly crossed his legs, hiding his rising interest.

Then she was up and poring over her ingredients, her face attractively flushed. He swallowed hard. She glanced his way.

He immediately discovered a fascinating ad in the magazine. She considered him long enough for him to grow self-conscious.

When she was safely absorbed again measuring and stirring, he set down the magazine and leaned back. He admired her. So what? It wasn't anything to be embarrassed over. She was one hell of a manager, strong in her convictions, not afraid to do what she thought was right. His admiration was thoroughly professional.

She was stirring something thick. Her breasts swayed slightly as she worked. Everett admired that, too, how she put her whole self into what she did.

Cool air brushed an unexpected part of his anatomy. He jerked a glance down. Professional admiration hell. He pushed his "admiration" between his crossed his legs and redraped his dressing gown. "Kirk, you've been without a woman way too long," he muttered.

"I beg your pardon?" Edie said.

"Uh, I said, I've been without a, uh, nap, too long." He lay his head on the back of the chair and closed his eyes. But it was a long, uncomfortable time before he got to sleep.

*

Everett woke to wonderful smells. His stomach rumbled appreciatively. "What's for dinner?"

"A little of this and a little of that." Edie smiled. "Come and eat."

What that curving smile did to her full pink lips… He nearly said what he'd like to eat was her and made an ass of himself. Clamping his stupid mouth shut, he made his way to the table.

He sat down to a veritable feast.

Edie had taken rice, oatmeal and fruit, the little of this and the little of that, and put together a miracle. Spiced rice pilaf, asparagus in a lemon-yellow sauce topped with slivered almonds, and steaming biscuits. And for dessert, she'd baked peach cobbler swimming in thick, sweet milk.

Everett surfaced from his food ten minutes later. "This is wonderful."

"I'm glad you're enjoying it," Edie said dryly. "Do you always inhale your dinner?"

Everett didn't even slow down. "I was hungrier than I realized. And this is wonderful."

"You said that."

"Yes." Everett delighted in the flavors mingling on his tongue. Most programmers he knew could barely find their way around the inside of the freezer. The hot biscuits and cobbler thawed something inside him. Anyone who made something this wonderful for him couldn't be the dark soul trying to destroy his career. "Because it's just so won—"

"Wonderful, yes, I know." Her fine, dark eyes were a little dull, the normally aggressive curls drooping slightly.

She must be tired. While he had napped, she had put her entire self into whipping up this miracle. "Why don't you go to bed? I can clean up."

She gave him an odd look. "There's only one bedroom."

"Yes." He spooned up the rest of the cobbler and ate it in two bites.

"There's only one bed."

Some remnants of cobbler remained in the pan. He pulled the pan in front of him and scraped until he'd gotten it all, then licked the spoon clean. He sat back with a satisfied sigh. "So you take the bed. I'll be fine on the chair."

"That's hardly equal, Kirk."

At that, his attention finally left his plate to focus on her. He wondered when he'd sunk back from Everett into Kirk. "I don't mind."

"I do." She rose to her feet. "I demand equality here."

Damn, what was wrong now? She was as prickly as second day whiskers. "Fuck equality." Everett tossed the spoon into the empty pan. It hit with a sharp clang. "You're tired. Take the bed."

"Don't swear." Her eyes grew wide and suspiciously bright, and her lip started quivering.

Everett was immediately contrite. "I'm sorry, Edie. I shouldn't have lost my temper. Edie?"

Strange liquid filled her fine dark eyes. His fireball was collapsing.

He jumped to his feet to gather her into his arms. Surprisingly, she wasn't the mountain he thought her, simply a woman, and a small one at that. He hugged her close. "Talk to me, sweetheart."

"Oh, Everett, I'm sorry." Dampness spread onto his chest, and her voice was a little thick. "I didn't really think we'd be here all night. I didn't think we could really be stranded. I guess I'm a little scared."

"Shh. It's okay." He rocked her gently. Kissed her head. Her hair was soft and sweet-smelling. "Don't cry."

She snapped away, wiping angrily at her eyes. "I'm not crying." Red rims belied her words. "I am perfectly capable of taking care of myself, whatever the circumstances."

"Of course you are." His voice came out softer than he meant. Less like an executive or even a colleague. More like a friend...or a lover. Someone who deserved to care. His face heated.

She clutched her elbows, reddening too. "I'll take the chair."

Everett sighed. This was one of those times that, even if he won, he'd lose. "Just for tonight. And I'll get some sheets for the couch. You'll get stiff in the chair."

Someday they'd compromise.

Compromise...like they'd both get the bed.

He didn't sleep well that night.

Chapter Six

Thanks for volunteering your ear. You're always there for me, and I want you to know I appreciate that. You said that sometimes it feels like you've known someone your whole life? I feel that way about you. As if I can tell you anything, and you'll still like me. I guess I'm a pretty sad person that an email address on the Internet can be one of my best friends.

But I have to tell someone. So here goes.

I have an enemy at work. He's trying to get rid of me. Or she. I don't know who it is, so I can't trust anyone here.

I can trust you though, right?

Thanks for letting me get this off my chest. I feel better already. You're a great friend, ED. The best.

—Prez

The cat growled at her. Edie pushed it away, her hand meeting empty air.

She came awake as her stomach growled again.

"Good morning." Everett sat in the living room chair, futzing with some rope. The past day came back, the door, the car ride, the bath, Everett's chest...

Kirk, not Everett. She needed the distance. Better yet, *Mr. Kirk. Mr. President Kirk.* "Morning." Her stomach growled again, nearly rip-sawing her esophagus. Stupid stomach, stupid morning, stupid president. Stupid snow. Stupid stuck car...a rich smell burned her nostrils. "Coffee?"

"I poured you a cup. It's beside you on the table."

He'd made coffee. Dear Kirk. Edie located the life-giving cup by feel. Dear *Everett*. She brought it to her nose—and seared her lungs. "What's in this?"

"Ground beans and a little water. The grinder was broken so I had to smash the beans with a hammer. No percolator either. I boiled it in a pan. It's hot, though. It'll wake you up."

"It'll peel the lining off my eyelids." Dutifully, Edie braved a gulp. It shaved off a third of her tongue. "Yeow."

"Good, hmm?" Everett dangled his work in front of him. It looked like a small noose.

"Good like a machete," Edie croaked. "What's that?"

"Animal snare. Not much food left so unless you're into bark and grubs, we'll have to catch something to eat."

"You're Tarzan now?"

"Sure." He beat his chest and yodeled.

"Yikes. Never do that again." Edie wrestled her way off the couch. She wondered if he really expected to catch anything with that wimpy snare. Hopefully not, because she really didn't want to eat the Easter Bunny or Bambi. "If you cook like you make coffee, I'd better do breakfast."

"Good luck. There isn't much left."

She paused. "I thought we'd be on our way home by now." She hurried into the kitchen to yank out frying pan and mixing bowl.

"Yes, you mentioned that last night." Everett's voice was even, but carefully so, as if he were working to keep understanding and sympathy out of it. Which only made it worse.

The little bit of flour left made a thin pancake batter. "I don't need your pity."

"Edie, the last thing in the world I'd do is pity you." He set his noose on the table. "Why don't you harangue me about the company's new coding standards?"

"I never harangue. But since you brought it up..." She poured batter. "Those 'standards' are absurd. They'll make the programmers unhappy. Happy employees produce more. Set the table, will you?"

He rose, lips twitching. He was, she realized, trying not to smile. Angry birds on a pogo stick, had he been baiting her?

"Edie, not everyone thinks like you do. If Bethany had to work under you for fifteen minutes she'd be miserable."

Edie slapped another pan onto a burner with more noise than necessary, added sugar and water and stirred vigorously over a high flame. "I don't see Ms. B. complaining when she has to work 'under' you."

"Ha-ha." He set out plates and forks. "All I'm saying is, not everything in life is black and white. Those cooked fast. Mine?" He smiled coaxingly.

Trolls take that hopeful little dimple. She slid the cakes onto his plate. She'd barely poured the next two when he raised the plate, empty again. "More?"

She wanted to keep up the wall of self-righteousness but he looked so cute. She not only flipped the next two cakes onto his plate, she splashed some hot, clear syrup from the other pan over them.

He cut a big square of double-decker pancake, blew on it, and put it into this mouth. His eyes closed as he chewed appreciatively.

At least this time he was chewing. Some deep part of her was strangely satisfied seeing him enjoy her cooking.

A deep, insane part. "It comes down to money, Everett. Workers are paid low wages and risk getting fired, while management walks away with their golden parachutes and inviolate bonuses."

His eyes opened. "Do you have a specific example or are you just flinging random accusations?" He held out his empty plate.

The ultimate male, handsome, arrogant, and boyishly appealing. All men should be drug out into the street and shot. Not really but it was annoying. And irresistible. She slid the next pair of cakes onto his plate. "Remember the wage cuts last year?" She scraped the last of the batter into the pan.

"Ten percent—but across the board. That's fair."

"Not really. What pared fat for the execs cut clerical to the bone. Then clerical wages were frozen so the people who needed it most never got it back." She flipped the cakes.

Everett swallowed and cast a longing look at the cakes in the pan. "They were eventually unfrozen."

"Stop with the puppy eyes." Edie sighed and slipped one pancake onto his plate. "Problem was, you executives had a *fifteen* percent raise three months before the ten percent cut. Giving you an overall raise."

He stiffened. "We can't help when the review structure places our raises."

Edie sat opposite Everett with her single pancake. "That sounds like Junior."

"Don't call him Junior. Is that all you're eating?"

"He's son of the chairman, isn't he?" Edie dribbled the teaspoon of syrup left onto her pancake. "This is all that's left. You ate the rest."

Everett dropped his fork with a clatter, his face going pale. "Edie, you should have said something. I'd never allow you to starve—"

"We're a long way from starving, Everett." She made short work of the cake. "And really, I'm having too much fun arguing with you."

"Fun?" The color washed back into his face and the dimple made a brief appearance. "Me too. And between us, I agree with your views on Junior."

"You're kidding."

"Sarcasm again?" Everett rose to take his dishes to the sink. "Where'd you pick up your views, Uncle Jake?" He stoppered the sink and poured hot water from the kettle in.

"My grandparents, mostly. But my management ideas?" She shrugged. "That's Philip."

Everett turned from squirting dish soap. "Is Philip your dad?"

"Like a father. Director of MIS at my first job. Big into office politics, workers' rights."

"Sounds like a great guy." Everett's tone was strangely sour as he ran cold water into the sink.

Edie shook her head, bringing her dishes to the sink. "He has his faults."

"Oh?" Everett raised a brow, a nonverbal "tell me more." Maybe he was actually trying to understand her. Like a friend.

A man as smart and powerful as Everett Kirk, caring enough to understand her? Wow. Like Philip. But this time she was without the misconception that it would last.

"Remember, you asked. A woman at my first job was fired for getting pregnant."

Everett cranked off the water. "Just for getting pregnant?" His expression was dark with outrage.

"By one of the company execs. The father wanted it to remain secret and she had the bad manners to threaten him with telling." Edie watched Everett's face. Now his indignity would turn against the unfortunate Aurora.

"She had the guts to tell? Good for her." He started washing. "They caught the guy?"

She stared at him. No alien burst from his chest. "Well, no. She was hustled out before she could say a word. No one heard from her again, so I suppose they did something to keep her from talking."

"That's illegal." Everett scrubbed the plate so hard it nearly broke. "I've seen it happen though. No one does a thing."

"I did."

His silver-blue eyes glinted. "I just bet you did. Marched into your supervisor's office, clue bat swinging?" He rinsed the plate and slid it into the strainer.

"Sort of, except it was the company president and I wasn't nearly so subtle. I said I'd report him."

"Good for you."

"Bad for me." She snatched up a drying towel, plucked up the plate and scoured it dry. "I didn't have any real plans for who to report him to. And…I kind of called him names, which got me fired too. I didn't do anyone any real good. It was…I was…" She hugged the plate to her chest. "It was dumb."

"Edie, you stood up for what you believed was right. That's good in my book." He gave her a quizzical look. "Someone told you that, didn't they? That it was dumb."

How did he know? "Well… Yes."

"That *Philip*?"

The sheer anger in Everett's voice startled her. Anger, on her behalf? "Philip would have played it smarter." She set the plate on the table and started on a plastic tumbler. "He'd have worked behind the scenes and made a real difference."

"That's not necessarily smarter. This Philip sounds good in theory but squeamish doing the real work. At least you had the guts to act."

She looked into Everett's eyes. The anger had melted into something warm, something like…admiration? She nearly fell into their glowing depths. "Everett…"

His eyes dropped to her lips, darkened.

She leaned toward him.

His head bent.

Her eyes closed and… The tumbler slipped from her hands, hitting the floor with a sharp crack. Her eyes flew open.

He jerked straight, cheeks ruddy. "Well. Those snares won't lay themselves." He tossed the washrag, swept on his coat and scarf, and left.

The cabin was quiet. Edie picked up the tumbler and finished drying the dishes.

He said she *hadn't* been stupid. How amazing. He told her she had guts. Extraordinary.

When the kitchen was in order, she sat in the front room and picked up a magazine, but didn't read it. The quiet became empty instead of peaceful. Ten o'clock passed, eleven. Noon. Reluctantly, Edie admitted she missed Everett.

Missing the corporate president. Now that was really stupid.

So she went outside to chop wood.

Chapter Seven

To: ThePrez@serenityrangers.com
From: ED@mythicmail.com
Subject: Re: Friendship

Dear Prez,

I'm honored that you feel that way about me. I care about the people I work with, but can't really bare my soul either, so I understand how it feels not to be able to talk over important things.

How terrible, to be forced out of your job! Worse if you don't know who's doing it. Is there anyone you suspect?

—ED

Late that afternoon Everett returned. His ponytail was crusted with ice and his cheeks were burnt red. He never looked so handsome to Edie.

"Where have you been all this time? Where did you go? How long does it take to lay out a few pieces of rope?" She fought to keep her voice level. Whack her with a laptop if he guessed that she'd missed him.

She also kept her throbbing leg carefully out of his sight.

"It takes," he pulled his stiff coat cuff back with difficulty to look at his watch, "about six hours."

Forgetting herself, she limped forward. "Why so long?"

Luckily he was turned, shedding his frozen outer garments, and didn't see. "I couldn't lay them too near the cabin. And I wanted to make sure there'd be game to trap. Mostly I was hunting spoor."

"You were looking for animal tracks? Did you find any?"

"After tramping for three hours, yes." He shot her a quick grin. "Seemed like I crossed the whole state. Really only a few miles but the snow slowed me."

"At least it's stopped." That grin blew her circuits. She forgot she was hiding her leg and limped to a kitchen chair.

In two strides, Everett was at her side. "What the hell did you do to yourself?"

She fell into the chair, surprised at his vehemence, and then crossed her leg to cover the rusty stain on her thigh. "Please don't swear."

"What. Did. You. Do."

Was that concern blazing in his eyes? "Nothing. Hardly anything. Really, Everett."

"'Nothing' does not make you limp. Take off your pants." He spun from her to stride to the sink.

"Take off my…? You may be my boss, Everett, but that doesn't allow you every liberty."

He jerked on the water and briskly washed his hands. "Edith Ellen Rowan, if you can tell me with a straight face that red lake on your jeans is not blood, then fine. If, however, for any reason I am not convinced—" He glared at her. "I will personally cut you out of them. Do I make myself clear?"

"Really, Everett, there's no need to become alarmed—"

"Take off the damned pants!"

Red-faced, Edie slipped out of her jeans. Nearly had a seizure when she saw what Freudian imp had dressed her this morning. Bend her over and whack her repeatedly with that laptop—red silk bikini panties?

Everett turned off the tap with his wrist. He was red-faced too, but the color on his high cheekbones might still be from the cold outside. Or the cold inside. The fire had burned out and the room's temperature had dropped.

He turned from the sink. Saw her. His eyes blazed with sudden ferocious heat.

She might have whimpered. He might have throttled a gut-deep groan.

He shook his head. Closing his eyes, he inhaled a bushel of air. Released it slowly.

When he opened his eyes, the heat was banked. With a rueful smile he came to kneel next to her and his big body radiated all the fierce heat on her naked skin that he'd throttled from his eyes. She squirmed on the chair.

His fingers were cool and gentle examining her, tenderly removing the half-dozen small sticky bandages she'd thrown on in an attempt at self-ministration. She forced herself to relax, not to react to his silky smooth touch on her thigh, his breath warming her flesh… Her red panties dampened. She clamped her thighs tight.

"How did you get this?" he asked softly.

The panties? No, he meant the wound. "We ran out of firewood. So I found an old ax around back—"

"I think I see where this is leading. No wonder the gash is so big. I'm surprised it didn't bleed more."

She'd have to hide the towel.

"Let's get you clean." He scooped her up.

Her stomach swooped as suddenly, easily, she was six feet off the ground. Her arms wrapped tight around his neck. "I can walk, you know." His silky hair feathered under her arm. Cool air brushed her panties. If he could smell her arousal like she could… She wanted to hide.

"I wouldn't survive seeing you walk in that sexy scrap of silk." He settled her onto the kitchen counter top, her thigh over the sink. "Stay here."

She bit her lip. He wasn't embarrassed for her? He was actually… interested? She did a quick survey of the room, but there weren't any body-snatcher pods either.

He started the kettle and went into the back hallway. A moment later, he returned with acetaminophen, a glass of water, several flat packages of gauze, and tape.

He handed her the glass and the acetaminophen. "Take two."

"You're taking this very well." She swallowed the pills.

"No reason to panic. You'll need to have this sewn up by a doctor when we get back. Maybe a tetanus booster as well."

"Don't panic, he says, in the same breath as 'needle' and 'shot.'"

"I didn't say the words. Only implied them."

"Uh-huh. Then I only have implied panic setting in."

His lips quirked as he tested the kettle water. "Good. Warm but not too hot."

"Shouldn't it boil?"

"We boiled it this morning." He poured the water over her thigh. It was soothing, until he added the soap.

"Ouch! Hey, that hurts."

"The medical term is sting." He swabbed on disinfectant.

"Holy hard drives, that sucker *stings*."

"Sting is good. Means it's getting clean." He rinsed her thigh gently, patted it dry, and covered it with gauze squares.

"Thank you, Nurse Kirk." She smiled.

He returned her smile. She fell into eyes as beautiful as a clear mountain stream... He bound the gauze with white tape.

"Tight." She wriggled. "Too tight."

"No, no, it's called 'pressure.' But I'll loosen it a bit." He cut the tape and wrapped it again.

The "pressure" receded. "More Serenity Rangers wisdom?"

"My mother the nurse. She insisted I learn first aid."

"Mmm." Warm and comfortable now, she felt cared for. Happy. "Thank you, Everett."

"I get a thanks and a beautiful smile? Play with sharp things as often as you like."

She drew herself straight. "Really, Everett, I wasn't playing."

"I know." He lifted her from the sink, making her stomach

swoop again—really, he was immensely strong—and settled her on the couch, placing a blanket over her. "You were contributing to our well-being, and I appreciate it."

"Maybe I should say thank you more often."

"Nah. You'll spoil me." He sat beside her, caressed a finger over her cheek.

Her eyes closed, her entire being concentrated on that sweet touch. Her body fired up, her lips started throbbing… The touch, his heat was gone. Her eyes opened.

He was at the door, throwing on his coat. He'd grabbed the ax from where she'd hidden it behind the chair. "You're right, we need more firewood. I'd better get chopping." His voice was strained. "Save some of those bandages for me."

*

The instant the door clicked shut she threw off the blanket and limped to the window. Though Everett appeared competent, he was still an executive, more used to commanding than doing. If she'd sliced her thigh, no telling what trouble he might get into with that ax.

He disappeared into the woods.

"Sweet pickled motherboards. What does that man think he's doing?" She limped back and forth until her thigh ached. She sat down, but less than ten minutes later popped up again and scurried to the window.

Everett was returning with a freshly cut tree.

She pressed her face to the cold glass. He'd found a handsaw. He trimmed branches and sectioned the tree into several logs.

He placed the first log on the chopping block. Hefted the ax.

Edie sucked in a breath. Said the only word that truly covered this situation. "Damnation!" She grabbed her coat to run out and stop him.

Everett split the log with one clean chop. Edie froze, flabbergasted.

Then Edward Everett Kirk, company president and CEO, started cleaving wood rhythmically as if he did it every day of his life. Pick up the log, swing the ax, split the log. Repeat. Edie hung up her jacket and settled in by the window to watch.

He stopped after four logs to remove his coat. He was only wearing a T-shirt, idiot man, did he want to get sick…?

He hefted the ax. Edie's breath imploded.

Muscles sprang out of nowhere. The damp tee clung to the tops of his chest, the pinpoints of his nipples, the breadth of his shoulders. His back flared like a cobra as he swung the ax around and high overhead. Powerful shoulders brought the ax down, sinews in his forearms springing into relief as he completed the split.

Edie stumbled away from the window, fell onto the couch. Panted shallow breaths.

Even shallow breaths stopped when Everett shouldered the door open, carrying an armload of wood.

Escaped strands of chestnut hair fell roguishly over forehead and cheek. His torso was thick with muscle. He looked like a woodland god striding into the cabin. She wanted to clasp his knees and pay homage to his… Spank her with a rack of panpipes. Hard. Repeatedly…she groaned.

"What's wrong?" He dumped his load by the wood burner, and then took one look at her leg and tutted. "You've been up."

"No. Maybe a little." She flushed and it wasn't embarrassment.

"You're not a very good liar." After washing his hands, he returned to the couch with more gauze and tape and settled next to her. His weight dented the cushion. She slid into contact with him, the heat of his body inflaming her. As he repaired her bandaging, one errant chestnut lock fell across his intent, serious face.

She reached up and brushed it back.

He looked at her, eyes abnormally bright.

Awareness sprang between them.

Slowly, he set aside paper wrappings and tape, gaze never leaving her face. She raised herself on her arms, yearning toward him.

He cupped her chin in his square, competent hand. She leaned into his fingers, eyes fluttering shut.

They kissed.

His lips were warm on hers, fluid, tasting her gently. Edie sighed. She tasted him in return, mint, fresh air, pine and all male.

His arms came around her, securing her against him, his tee wet but his body steaming hot. Her hands framed his face, palms sliding over his chiseled cheeks into his sleek hair, urging him closer. Groaning, he deepened the kiss. "You taste wonderful."

Edie's muscles melted. "Everett…why?"

"What?" He trailed kisses along her jaw.

"Why haven't you done this before?"

"Kiss you?" His lips chased fire down her neck. "I wanted to."

"Why didn't you?" Edie arched against his mouth. He nipped the tender skin of her throat. Her languidness flamed into something more passionate. More dangerous.

"The company," he nipped gently until she shivered, "doesn't allow relationships between employees."

"What?" Edie came bolt upright on the couch. "You wanted to kiss me but didn't because *the company wouldn't let you?*"

Everett rocked back, his eyes wide. "Well, not exactly—"

"Because the damned board didn't approve? Does the board issue you potty passes too?"

"Don't get crude."

"Crude? What's cruder than the company controlling private lives? Big Brother lives, he spies, and worse, he censors any emotion at all!"

"Edie, sweetheart. There are good reasons for discouraging personal relations—"

"So forget team building exercises! Might be misconstrued as a 'relationship.'"

"That's not it." Everett pushed back his straggling hair with a short, sharp shove. "Consider the repercussions. What if I asked you to dinner? Hell, what if I dated you? Your raises and promotions would be tainted with accusations of favoritism. Someone in the company, or even your team, would call you a brown-nosed bi—"

"Language!" Edie sprang off the couch. "My team is interested in honest personal relations. If I dated you, they'd know it was because I loved—" Her mouth hung open in horror.

"Damn it Edie." His eyes were on her thigh. "You've started bleeding again. Lay down, *now*."

He hadn't heard. Edie fervently thanked the Omega Point and meekly lay down.

Love. Where had that come from, anyway? He wasn't the complete enemy butthead she'd thought, but that didn't mean they were compatible.

In fact, they were opposites. They went together like gunpowder and a match. No, no! Like a hot fiery brand thrust into oil... Her body convulsed with pleasure.

Okay, sure, fine. They were *physically* compatible. But a devastating chest in a wet T-shirt and the fun she had arguing with him and his kindness tending her cut were rather shallow reasons to fall for a man. Which she *hadn't*.

Fussing over her bandage, Everett apparently hadn't noticing her silence. "Now stay put. I'll make dinner."

"Dinner? Out of what, your executive command?" Her words held no real heat.

"I'll find something." He rummaged in the cupboards.

She figured he'd have as much luck finding dinner as she would figuring out her annoying, misguided heart.

Chapter Eight

To: ED@mythicmail.com
From: ThePrez@serenityrangers.com
Subject: Re: Re: Friendship

See, I was right! If I told anyone here at work I was teetering on the edge of disaster, they'd be happy to give me the final push. But you truly care.

Who's trying to get me? The most obvious candidate is a woman who makes constant trouble. Except I can't believe it's her. I like her. A lot.

There's the man I replaced—no love lost between us. Not to mention his girlfriend, who's as political an animal as he is.

I'd appreciate your perspective on this, ED. I don't know which way to turn anymore.

—Prez

Edie sat on the couch, watching Everett evaluate their meager fare. He did it competently, as he did everything: his chopping wood, his caressing hands, his beautiful hot...throw her to the mat with kung phooey.

She reminded herself that Everett wasn't the epitome of masculinity. Well, he was, but...Philip would have handled this situation just as well as Everett. Wouldn't he? Philip was outdoorsy too, with his big truck and bigger house in the country...well, no. Philip's house wasn't rustic in the least.

She'd only been to his house once, back when he was first grooming her for management. High atop a hill, back deck extended over a breathtaking two-story escarpment, Philip's house screamed new construction. A carpet-like lawn (probably peeled away like a carpet too) held a life-sized statue of a spectacularly endowed but not particularly well-sculpted Greek goddess. Hopefully the stone wasn't marble since the artistry wasn't quite up to forever.

Philip met Edie with a glass of French champagne. "How do you like the landscaping?"

"Magnificent." Edie meant it but secretly preferred her grandparents' small roses and herb patch.

"Speaking of magnificent, let me introduce you to the wife." He escorted her into a house that was as overdesigned as an aging star with too many facelifts.

A blonde detached herself from a couple guests. Bee-stung lips curved in a smile that was friendly, for a realtor—or a buzz saw. "You must be Edie. I'm so glad you could come. I'm Petra." She shook Edie's hand with a two-handed grip. Three carats of diamond flashed.

"Nice to meet you." Edie kept her eyes glued to Petra's. From the neck down, Philip's wife was the model for the Greek goddess on the lawn.

"There are a few people Phil and I want you to meet—the right kind of people." Petra led the way to a buffet table laden with shrimp cocktail and *pâté de fois gras*, barbecued pheasant wings and creamed artichoke hearts, enough rich food to harden the arteries of an entire small country.

"Time to network," Philip murmured in Edie's ear. Petra smiled her brilliant, cutting smile.

That was when Edie knew she'd never fit into Philip's mold for her. Oh, she recognized the value of socializing. But she'd never quite gotten the hang of working the room.

"Food," Everett called.

Edie shook herself. She got up and hobbled to the table. "Dinner?"

"A handful of spaghetti and a bag of hardened raisins. Some dinner." Everett looked glum. "Oh yeah, and dessert—two granola bars."

In contrast to Philip Sedgwick's cornucopia, Everett's table looked clean and wonderfully ascetic. Edie patted his arm. "Well done, considering there wasn't anything left. Oh, you found salt!"

"Goodie, now we won't sweat to death."

She hid a smile. Poor Mr. President. "You did the best you could."

"As far as I can tell, you made a feast out of old shoes and cobwebs. I made spaghetti and raisins."

"Nouveau cuisine." Edie sat and wolfed down her food in less than a minute. She pushed away, patting her belly. "I needed to lose weight anyway."

"Hardly." Everett scowled. "If you get any thinner they'll hoist flags on you."

"Such a lovely compliment."

"Well..." Everett's lips quirked. "They'd have to be very short flags."

"Even lovelier." Edie smiled back encouragingly. He might irritate her in the extreme but she didn't like seeing him unhappy. "What about you? Are you still hungry?"

"Of course not. How could I fail to thrive on my own cooking?" Everett's stomach let out a loud growl, contradicting him. He rose from the table and took the dishes to the sink, reached for the dish soap and then let his hand fall. "Let's leave these for later."

"Fine with me." Edie rose, started to limp toward the couch.

"Stay off that leg." Everett swooped in, scooped her up easily, and carried her to the couch.

So fast. So strong. It left her breathless. She blinked at him.

His focus was on her mouth.

He was going to kiss her again.

Her belly lurched. She wanted that. Wanted his mouth on hers, his talented lips melting her, his thrusting tongue making her helpless with desire... Yet she shouldn't want him. They had no real future. It would only be sex. Except even corporate antagonists could learn to like each other...

While her mind was churning, his mouth closed on hers.

Silky lips moved with exactly the right firmness to coax her throbbing response. His mouth was so warm, moved so sweetly. Her eyelids fluttered shut. Her fingers slipped into his hair. His arms tightened on her, pulling her flush to him, waking her nipples, making her breasts tingle. Her bones liquefied.

His stomach let out a loud roar.

Her eyes flew open. "You *are* hungry."

He bit off a curse. "All right, yes. Starving." He lay her gently on the couch. Then he marched off to the sink, adding in a barely audible mutter, "The question is, what am I starving for?"

*

Edie hugged her knees. Everett was stalking the cabin like a caged lion. He stopped, stared at the dishes, and then stalked away to the wood burner to stare at it. He swung open the doors, jammed more wood inside, and shut the stove with a clang. Then he resumed his stalk, only to stare at something else.

She knew how he felt. Her lips were still tingling, her breasts aching, and she wanted him to kiss her again. To do much, much more. How crazy.

Edie sighed. "Would you stop that?"

"Stop what?"

"That pacing. It's making me nervous."

He reached the end of the cabin and started back. "I've got a headache. The pacing helps relieve it."

"Take an acetaminophen." She chafed her sore leg.

"You had the last one. Leave your cut alone."

She wanted him to kiss her, *he* wanted to mother her. "Sure, blame your headache on me."

"I'm not blaming it on you." Everett halted, face grim. "I'm perfectly aware that if we had taken your car, or I had stopped somewhere safe, or at least asked directions, we wouldn't be in this fix. That *you* would be safe and whole."

Perversely, that made her want to defend him. "If we'd left when you wanted us to we'd have made it safely to the motel."

"If I didn't eat so damn much, we'd have plenty of food." Everett's voice rose.

"If I didn't cook so damn much, you wouldn't have eaten it all!" She wanted to kiss him and damn the stupid company policy and his stupider self-discipline.

"Don't swear." Everett started pacing again. "At least I'm doing something about it."

"You swear. Why can't I? What are you doing, the snares? You can't possibly expect to catch anything."

"Of course I expect to catch something. Trust me. I wouldn't have spent all damn morning laying them if I didn't."

"No damn swearing if I can't. You are so stubborn. Delegate, Kirk!"

"Some things can't be delegated." He snatched up his coat and tugged it on. "Especially not to a stubborn firebrand who would rather cut off her leg than accept help!"

"Where do you think you're going?" Edie hopped off the couch, hobbled toward him.

"I'll show you I'm not playing. Stay down, damn it. We don't have many more bandages."

"Stop using that word, dammit." Fear pushed her into his personal space. Not fear. Anger.

"I'm not as creative as you are. What word do you want me to use, rats?"

She thrust toe-to-toe, so close she felt his blazing heat. Glared up. "Fine."

"Fine." He glared down. His eyes fired. His head lowered...
"*Rats.*" He spun for the door.

"Wait! Your jacket is still wet. It's freezing outside." She hobbled
after him.

He spun back. "Get back on the da...the *rats* couch."

"You're not—"

"*You* are." He took two strides, scooped her up and deposited
her on the couch, so she was. "Now stay the rats there!"

He stomped out.

She swore, jumped up and hopped to the window. He was long
gone. *Rats*, he was fast. How could he leave? Did he really believe
those bits of string would catch them breakfast? Ridiculous.

She hobbled back and forth, fretting. Waiting anxiously for her
man...*rats*.

She put the teakettle on, rummaged around for cup and tea,
and did *not* fret. Especially not about how they'd parted. The kettle
whistled. Why did they always end up arguing? She dropped the
teabag into the cup and poured. She wanted to argue with him
right now. If her leg weren't injured she'd be running after him to
have a good fight with him, the kind he deserved, where she could
grab him by the shoulders and scream in his face and then kiss
him and kiss him... She dunked the teabag so fast water sloshed
onto the table.

Idiot. She tossed the bag away.

Unless they fought *because* she was drawn to him, clashing like
two gears going different speeds. If they could find a common
speed, if they could ever *mesh*...

The sudden shock of need made her thighs clamp, her whole
body clench. She breathed through it. Compatible physically, oh
yes. Unfortunately oh yes.

But philosophically? He was from PC and she was from Mac.

Although...even committed lovers disagreed. It was significant
that, during the worst of their arguments, Everett never tried to

make her feel wrong or bad. He'd even taken her side a time or two in the HHE tug of war. She never admitted she knew, because he might be embarrassed.

She folded her hands around the hot cup. That wasn't true. What she couldn't admit was that Edith Ellen Rowan ever needed rescuing. How could her grandparents be proud of her then? She especially didn't want to admit that it was the Evil Overlord who rescued her. Then she might have to see him, not as Mr. President Kirk, but as a kind and generous man.

He might be embarrassed, right. She was the one who was embarrassed. He'd called it, all right—she didn't accept help very easily.

She owed him an apology. When he got back, she'd make it. What happened after, well, they'd see.

Mind set, conscience relieved, but body still throbbing and pent-up, she sat down with her tea to wait.

Chapter Nine

To: ThePrez@serenityrangers.com
From: ED@mythicmail.com
Subject: Problem spotted

It's that trouble-making woman. How can you like her? Believe me, I'm your friend. It's her, she's the one.

—ED

Edie woke cramped and aching, and automatically checked her phone for the time. Two thirty in the morning. What was she doing on the couch? It was her turn on the bed. They hadn't explicitly agreed to trade nights, and it would be hard for Everett to fit his great height on the couch. But it was only equal. She got up, shuffled to the sink, drew a glass of water, and shuffled into the bedroom.

The bed was empty.

"Everett?" Her voice rang through the cabin in a distressingly echoey way. She speed-hobbled from room to room, even going so far as to check under the couch. No Everett.

She hobbled to the door, swung it open. "Everett!" Snow blew into her face, her open mouth. She slammed the door shut and coughed. "Damn it, if you're not dead, I'm going to name you Bill and take a whole movie franchise to kill you."

Her aching leg benched her. She fretted on the couch past three, past three thirty. Enough was enough. Leg or no, she was going after him.

She'd just tossed on her jacket when the door swung open. A blast of cold air carried in a swirl of snow and a very white Everett.

Edie turned. "What the hell—"

"Thhatt's rats," he stuttered between pinched lips, staggering into the room like his legs were stilts.

"Where have you been?" She pushed the door shut behind him before attacking him with fussing, yanking off his ice-crusted coat and slapping the slush out of his hair a bit harder than necessary. "Where are your gloves?"

"Lost 'em. Dumb." A shiver passed through his big frame.

Edie grabbed his arm and guided him to the couch where she pushed him down and cocooned him in blankets. "Let me see your hands."

He poked them out of the cocoon.

She wanted to cry. His competent hands were dead white, along with his nose and the tips of his ears. "Damn it, you've got frostbite."

"R…rats. And n…no." Everett's words were accompanied by the castanets of his teeth. "N…not f..fr'ssbite."

"Of course not." Edie threw off her jacket and started the kettle. "Take off your shoes."

"Stupid." The word was huffed.

"And the rest." She grabbed a bucket and filled it from the tap. The water was just a few degrees from ice but it would feel like fire on his "not-frostbitten" feet. She glanced at him to see if he was following orders.

To her surprise, he was. Piece by sodden piece, clothes came out from under the huddled mountain of blankets. Everything was wet, even his undershirt—the thin white cotton that had molded so faithfully to his chest—

No. Now was not the time to provoke her pent-up, aching, heavily *throbbing*…phooey.

She lugged the bucket to the couch and stuffed his white feet in. Impressively, all he did was grimace.

The kettle whistled. She retrieved it and slowly poured hot water into the bucket. Gradually, his feet gained color. He sighed.

She left him to soak and made the rest of the hot water into tea. Before she let him drink, she lifted the mug to his mouth and blew its wafting steam into his lips until they were a healthy red. He really had the most kissable mouth... She tipped the mug so he could drink.

"Stupid," he muttered again.

"I'm stupid?"

"Me." He shifted under the blankets to take the mug from her. "I was out too long. But I don't have frostbite."

Edie stared his lips again, fascinated by the way they moved as he spoke. "What turned your feet white?"

"Frost*nip*. Frostbite leaves permanent damage. And hurts a hel—rats of a lot more."

She watched him talk, her fingers aching to caress his warm, moving...cry her a whole river of rats. She grabbed a washcloth and briskly took it to his feet instead.

"What hurts is my pride. The snares were empty."

"Not your fault." She scrubbed his feet until they were pink. "You can't control weather, or what animals do."

"I should be able to."

"What, you're a demigod now? Nice promotion."

His mouth quirked. "What can I say? HHE has great career opportunities. President, then demigod, then chairman of the board, where I get a quarter mil, a Lexus, and my own small planet."

Then he slumped. "But it's not godlike. It's simple planning, something I can usually do in my sleep." He clutched the mug. "I'm such an imbecile!"

"Perfectionist much?" Gently, Edie took his feet from the bucket, wiped them dry and laid them on the couch. Then she sat next to his feet and started massaging.

"We all have to have something to shoot for. Today perfection, tomorrow that small planet." He set down the mug, laid back and shut his eyes. Almost grudgingly he added, "That feels good."

"I'm glad." She switched feet, massaging each toe, then the ball, then using her knuckles on the side. "I heard from other people that you were hard on yourself at work. But I never saw it before this."

"Usually you're too involved in your own work."

"Meaning self-absorbed?" Edie started massaging up his calf, which was nicely taut and muscular. Time for her apology, but… if she admitted she was wrong, would he use it against her? The potential vulnerability scared her.

No, she trusted him. Time to prove it. "Maybe I've been a little blind. About the…office thing."

His eyes opened, a blue so deep she fell into them. He half-sat, reaching out to rasp a thumb over her cheek. The blankets dropped from his torso, revealing smooth skin over hard muscles—seen in her periphery because she was drowning in his eyes. "Edie, you're one of the most caring people I know. Sometimes it makes you single-minded. That's hardly a fault."

"You have all sorts of excuses for me, but you're hard on yourself." As if the blankets had also dropped from her eyes, she felt like she was truly seeing him for the first time.

"I'm not as selfless as you think." He cupped her face. "I'd like to kiss you, you know."

She thrilled to the words. "What about company policy?"

He sighed and dropped his hand. Shrugged the blanket back onto his shoulders. "I didn't make the rules. But when I took the job I agreed to carry them out."

"Poor Everett." Her fingers, still on his leg under the blanket, massaged slowly, gently past his calf to his thigh.

He groaned. "That feels better than good."

"But you don't just follow the rules, do you, Everett? If you did, I'd have been out the door years ago." The thick muscle delighted her fingers. She kneaded his thigh, working her way up.

"Edie. You're killing me." He stopped her hands with one of his.

She simply began massaging his competent hand. "What have you done for the little guy that I don't know about, Everett?"

Her massage wrung another groan from him, as well as the truth. "Jack."

"What about Jack?" She rubbed his strong forearm.

"He was on Bethany's team. He wasn't happy."

She stopped massaging to stare at him. "*You* moved him to my team?"

"Yes." Everett's eyes almost dared her to say something insulting.

"What else, Everett?" She slid her hands from under the blanket to massage his shoulders. She had to lean against his hard, hot chest, to get the proper leverage. Her fingers dug into rock-like deltoids. "Come on, tell me."

He groaned, said as if it were torn from him, "I had the wage freeze removed."

The freeze on the clerical staff, lowest on the corporate totem pole. No one cared about them except Edie...and now, she discovered, Everett. She crawled up his chest and whispered into his ear, "Why Everett, that was sweet." She brushed his lips with hers.

"Sweet?" He huffed. "Is Tarzan sweet? Are demigods sweet? I'll show you sweet." Wrapping his arms around her, he pulled her flat against him, his hard chest imprinting her. A hand clasped the back of her head. Holding her tight, he crushed his mouth down on hers.

Her belly furled with fiery delight. His tongue was hot wet velvet tracing her lips, flame thrusting between. Bright desire threaded her veins. She moaned and opened for him.

He seemed to have not only forgotten company policy, but thrown it headfirst into the snow. His big hands ranged along her back, down her spine, cupping her hips, kneading. Returning to slide under her waistband. She could have stopped him at any point, but his touch was magical. By the time he dipped into the dimples of her derriere, fingers teasing the whisper of hair, she was limp with need.

He sat and shifted her onto his lap. She wiggled against the thickness pressing up under his blanket. Either his boxers were made by the old Soviet tank division, or he was savagely aroused. She thrilled to it.

Briefly she worried about the frostbite. But his body was hot and his mouth had started nibbling laps down her neck and she didn't want to stop because when would he ever forget himself enough to do this again? She squirmed harder against him, raising his physical interest until the blankets slithered off and...good freaking genie-rubbing lamps.

He was naked.

Far from weakening or embarrassing him, it added a fierce edge to his masculinity. "Edie, my fireball, let me touch you." His tongue dipped into the notch of her throat, breath billowing against her skin.

She didn't trust herself to answer. She took his hand and guided it under her shirt. He winnowed under her bra, cupped and kneaded and finally pinched until she moaned and strained into him. Until she grabbed his head and pulled.

With one swift tug, he raised her shirt and bra and set to suckling her nipple. He drew hard, his mouth fiery hot. Her feet curled. Her fingers raked through his hair, demolishing the civilized ponytail. Loose chestnut strands cascaded through her hands. She gloried in the feel of it, raw silk and heat.

She threw her shirt off. Straddling him, she grabbed his head again, holding him to her breast. "Make love to me, Everett."

His hands caressed her, his mouth roved over her. "Edie. Sweetheart. I can't."

"What?" It took a moment. "What do you mean?"

He feasted on her like a starving man. "I can't make love to you."

She pulled away. His erection was still raging under her, so that wasn't the problem... Then she knew, and was outraged. "Company policy, Kirk?" She jumped off him. Stared at his hips, her eyebrows lifting. No, *that* wasn't the problem at all.

"Edie, no." He groaned, his arms out as if they still held her.

"Then what?" Had he remembered she was the worker drone enemy? She bit back her tears, armored herself in anger. "You're too good for me?"

"No, sweetheart." He opened eyes clouded with passion...and confusion. "I just don't have protection."

"What protection?"

"No condom." He cheeks went ruddy. "That pregnant woman and her boss...I don't want even the echo."

"Oh." Edie paled. "I beg your pardon. You're right, of course. Thank you. That's...considerate." She hugged herself, turning away. "It's your turn on the couch tonight."

"Yes, of course." A pause. "Good night, Edie." His voice was soft.

She made for the bedroom, her leg—and other parts—throbbing. The bed was cold.

Chapter Ten

To: ED@mythicmail.com
From: ThePrez@serenityrangers.com
Subject: Re: Problem spotted

Dear ED,

I'd think you sound jealous, but that's impossible—you don't even know if I'm the opposite sex! No worries. I like this woman a lot...and maybe even more than like her...but I don't trust her. Well, I do trust her, actually. But even if you were jealous, you'd have nothing to worry about, because she doesn't like me. Not like I like her. She's always fighting me, when she's not ignoring me or worse.

What I'm trying to say is that *you* are my friend. Please believe that, ED.

—Prez

Monday morning Edie woke in a strange bed, weak sun high in the sky. Her head ached and her eyes stung and her heart hurt and she remembered the near miss lovemaking with Everett.

Not lovemaking. Sex. She threw back the covers and got dressed.

He'd stopped because he didn't want them to end up like Aurora and Leadbottom. Sweet, caring...and annoying. Everett had a wild, sensual side that Edie liked. A lot. She'd like to see a lot more of it.

Her grandparents would also like Everett's wild child when she brought him home to meet them...

She had not just thought that.

The instant she left the bedroom she felt the cabin's emptiness. "Rats! Scourges and plagues of rats!"

He was gone again. His coat couldn't have dried out all that much in a few hours. "Frostnip my cute ass. The man is an amputation waiting to happen."

She didn't even think about her gashed leg, just threw on her coat and jammed her feet into her boots. He'd gone outside with frostbite, barehanded since he'd lost his gloves. The man's skull must be full of dancing hamsters. Like refreezing thawed meat, frostbite was way worse the second time.

She thought of Everett without those fine hands, and nearly cried. Throwing open the door she sucked in a breath to shout his name. The air froze her lungs and her eyebrows froze. When had frigid become WTF? No wonder Everett had looked so ghastly. She had to find him. She slammed the door shut and dug into her clothes bag. Extra pants lined her jeans, another pair of socks insulated her feet. She wound a scarf around her head and jammed a hat over that. Better prepared, she went outside.

Everett's tracks led away from the cabin. She followed them through a stand of trees into a large clearing, dismayed to see them trail far into the distance. Damn his provider-instinct hide. She wanted to find him before he was so frozen that she'd have to ride him back like a sled. Although if she turned his hard body over she could ride him other ways…whip her with Cat 5, when had she gotten so sex-on-the-brain?

The cold quickly tired her but she pressed on. At least her aching leg no longer ached, numb now. That was good news, wasn't it? Probably not, but she wasn't going to let it stop her.

She lost his trail, backtracked, and found a barely perceptible path. Ten minutes passed, and twenty. Her breath froze her nostrils raw. The snow swam before her eyes.

How had Everett made this trek, not once or twice, but three times?

The path wound into a thick stand of firs. There she lost his trail entirely. She plowed forward, frantic, hoping to rediscover it on the other side but when she broke through the trees there was nothing but pristine snow.

She scrambled back the way she had come, her breath quick steamy puffs. The last clear prints were at the edge of the forest. She bent, hands on knees, chest aching, eyes swimming...spots. On the snow.

She dropped to her knees. Dark red spattered the snow around Everett's footprints. She jerked off one glove to touch it. It was cold. She took a pinch of red snow and rubbed it between her fingers. When it warmed, it was sticky. She raised her trembling hand to her nose and sniffed. Flinched.

Blood.

"Everett," she screamed. It rang on the crystal-cold air.

She ran, vectoring from the prints through the trees, out into a clearing. Still no tracks but she kept plowing forward, up a steep incline, anger and fear pushing her to crest the top.

Pain seared her thigh, knifed her side. She pressed hands to her flank and paused, panting in shards of brittle air. She peered through ice-crusted slits.

A dashed trail broke the blanket of snow. Man-sized. She stumbled forward, her heart pumping in her throat.

A cry shattered the frigid air. She stopped dead in her tracks.

Scuffling. Twigs cracking. A high-pitched squeal, a deep grunt. A shout.

Everett.

She half-skated, half-stumbled down the hillock's slick crest. Hitting bottom unexpectedly she fell. Snow thrust past her cuffs to freeze her wrists. She scrabbled to her feet, shaking it out.

A shriek split the air. Animal? Human? She followed the dashed trail as fast as she could.

She burst through a ring of scrubby pines. Across the clearing of packed and churned snow, crouched beneath far boughs, was Everett. She almost didn't recognize him.

His face was flushed, his hair completely loose. His eyes glittered through the curtain of chestnut hair like those of a wild thing.

He saw her and straightened, triumphantly holding up a string of rabbit carcasses. She could practically feel the primitive masculine waves coming off him.

"You did it." She was a little awed. "You caught something with those bits of string. Congratulations." She started toward him, casually, as if she hadn't been searching frantically for the past hour.

He grinned. "The animals finally came out."

That boyish grin did it. She ran the last few feet and threw herself at him. He dropped his prey and caught her easily.

"Oh, Everett! I thought you were dead…or frozen in the ice… or worse."

"Not cold in the least, not chasing after this bugger." Setting her down, he picked up one unstrung rabbit. "He worked the noose loose and scampered around the whole dratted clearing before I got him."

"I heard." She insinuated herself back into his arms. "Yelling, shrieking…I wasn't sure if it was you."

"Him, mostly. Animals can make a bloody racket." His warm lips found her hair.

"I saw blood." She shuddered.

"Him again. But I could use a bath. I'll tell you about it on the way back."

She braced away from him, searching his eyes. "I didn't believe you could do it."

"Is that an apology?" He dimpled. His handsome face, flushed with success and framed by swirling chestnut hair, dazzled her.

"Yes," she said softly.

"I'm mostly a city boy, but there is more to me." He smiled into her eyes.

She traced the small scar on his chin. "I'm beginning to realize that. Did you get this hunting rabbits?" Shyly she added, "I've always wondered."

"Have you?" Gently he disentangled her. "Let's go back to the cabin. I can tell you the story on the way." He picked up the game and headed off.

She trotted along in his wake. It was easier going with his feet packing the way. Her leg was barely throbbing. "That scar's not recent, is it?"

"Fifth grade. Top grade in my elementary school."

"What happened?"

"I was on safety patrol. One spring day, this spindly little first-grader was waiting on my corner to cross. Three seventh-grade types skidded up on dirt bikes, spitting mud from the gutter. Mud splattered everywhere, and a pebble hit the poor first-grader in the face. I called the seventh graders on it, but they just jeered.

"They probably would have ridden on, and that would've been the end of it. But the neighborhood I grew up in…we had gangs. This first-grader was wearing the wrong colors. The trio dropped their bikes and grabbed the kid to beat him up."

"Everett, how horrible! How badly was he hurt?"

"Not at all. I seized the biggest asshole by the collar and yanked him off. When the jerk tried to plant his fist in my face, I introduced him to the sidewalk. Anyway, not to bore you, I managed to convince those bullies that they didn't want to pick on smaller kids. This scar was my trophy."

"I get the feeling that's not all there is to the story."

"Really? Why?" Everett shot her a look of pure innocence over his shoulder.

"A fifth grader besting three big middle schoolers? You must have had some sort of weapon. Iron knuckles? Mace?"

"Those are illegal, Ms. Rowan. No, I had one very basic weapon that made me unstoppable. I was willing to get hurt fighting for that little kid. They weren't."

They walked in silence after that. She hadn't known him at all. She was impressed with him, fighting for that unknown first grader all those years ago. She suspected he still fought so wholeheartedly for the little guy today.

Chapter Eleven

To: ThePrez@serenityrangers.com
From: ED@mythicmail.com
Subject: Are you a mind-reader?

I was about to respond in a perfectly rational but snippy email that I was definitely *not* jealous of the woman you like a lot.

A lot. You like her *a lot*.

And then I realized you were right, I am jealous, although not quite the way you think. Despite fighting, you still like her. There's a man...I want so much to be liked by him. He fights and ignores me as much as your woman fights and ignores you. But I still want his trust and respect. I want him to like me for myself, even the imperfect parts of me.

That irritating man, I spend all my time thinking about him. Well, I guess that's the definition of irritating :D

But I'm happy to know *you* like me, Prez. Hey, you tolerate my awful computer jokes—we must be made for each other :)

—ED

Back at the cabin, Everett disappeared into the bedroom and emerged minutes later, hair neatly tied back, black sweater obscuring his powerful torso, baggy slacks civilizing his muscular legs.

Edie looked up from her magazine. "I liked you better the other way. You're going to get that nice outfit messy cleaning the rabbits."

He threw a flannel shirt on over his sweater. "I suppose it's too much to ask you to clean them?"

"I'll cook, Everett, but you have to do the Tarzan stuff."

"Ha. I get to be Tarzan after all." Everett rolled up his sleeves, fished a knife and meat cleaver out of the drawers and spread newspaper on the table.

"As long as you don't yodel."

"Killjoy." He sat down with the first carcass. "By the way. This is game, so if you're cooking, make sure to cook it well. Don't want to get—"

"Tularemia?"

He looked up in surprise. "You like this wilderness thing, then?"

"Well, yes. It's so different from civilization." Edie set the magazine aside and watched his hands, competent, efficient. "This is life or death. Exciting. Dangerous."

"What if I told you HHE is more dangerous than any wilderness?"

"I'd ask what hallucinogen you're on. And if you could get me some."

"Think about it. Clients are the prey the company has to hunt to survive." Gestures with his knife punctuated his remarks. "Corporate infighting determines pecking order, like a wolf pack. Sometimes survival itself is threatened."

"No way. Suits, ties and pantyhose are not wild kingdom."

"I disagree. Corporate politics are more savage than any horror of Mother Nature's. Howell Senior hired me to supplant his own son. What sire in nature would bring in an outsider to lead the pack? And then there's Bethany. Why do you think she's having an affair with Howell?"

"Because they're two of a kind?"

"Think stallion."

Edie blushed.

"Bethany wants power." Everett started filleting. "In addition to her own position, being Howell's lover confers power on her. Like a lead mare."

"That's awfully sexist. And I still don't buy it. What about your hand-tailored shirts and Italian shoes? Those are pure civilization."

"Are they? How does nature protect the puffer fish? Why dapple the coat of a fawn?"

She gaped at him. "You're saying power ties and gold watches are protective coloration?"

"Exactly." He dumped the meat into the pot, washed his hands. "Screaming to the competition, 'I'm bigger and I'm stronger. Don't mess with me.'"

"Then the man I see at the office, he's not you at all?"

"Oh, he's part me. But not, I think, the best part. That's you." He came to her and took her face between clean palms. "You're the part that fights for the employee and tells the truth no matter how damning. The part that doesn't play corporate games, the part that has big brown eyes to live in and sweet soft lips to die in…" He bent his head and kissed her.

His mouth teased, tasted. Warmth stole over her like hot mulled wine, tingling down her throat, pooling in her belly. His tongue touched her lips, slid between. Eagerness flared and she pressed into him. He deepened the kiss, fingers tangling in her hair.

When she was dazed and panting, he lifted his head. "Edie, my fireball. You're the one who both civilizes me and makes me wild." His fingers drifted lightly over her face, her neck, his touch like velvet. "You can stop me any time, you know."

"Not happening." She wrapped herself around him and pulled, toppling them both onto the couch. While she could still think, she freed his hair.

Her fingers ran through raw silk, reveling in untamed length. She curled strands in her fingers and pulled his head to her, kissing him hungrily. He groaned and opened his mouth on her and they kissed each other, give and take, tongues tumbling and teeth nipping.

His hands skimmed her breasts, thumbing her nipples through cloth. She shivered. Her need spoke through her hands, urging his head down her body.

He shoved her sweater and bra up, baring her breasts. His warm lips found her nipple and suckled. She arched against the couch, gasping with her ripening desire.

"Soon, sweetheart." He laved her nipple, and then gave equal attention to the other until both her breasts were throbbing and tight. Her fingers dug so deep in the silk of his hair that she thought she might be attached to him forever, wrapped in deliciously warm, seductive strands, wrapped in *Everett*...the idea didn't scare her as much as it should have.

He kissed a warm trail down her middle. Sparkles followed. His hair slid from her hands; she clutched the couch instead.

As he went, he pulled off her doubled pants and underwear in one long tug. His lips burned a long path down the smooth skin of her thigh. "Edie, my fireball. My heart. Open for me."

She ached so much. Parting her knees seemed her only relief. Her legs fell open. Cool air brushed her dewy center, almost immediately replaced by his fiery hot palm. He cupped her vulva and rode it gently with his hand while he kissed her belly, her mons. "Tell me what you want, Edie. Tell me how you like it."

No one had ever asked her before. But with Everett it seemed perfectly natural to tell him *that* felt very nice, that *this* made her shudder, and when he did them both together it made her want to scream. So he did them both together and she did scream and burst and fluttered down into absolute peace.

Eyes shut, she said, "Now you."

His only answer was a groan.

"Problem?"

"Unless you can make condoms out of rabbit guts, I have the same problem as before.

"*We* have the problem, Everett." She opened her eyes. "But there are ways around it."

And while the meat simmered slowly, she proceeded to show him some of the things that she'd learned since her commune days.

*

When Everett was boneless under her, Edie rested her head on his muscled thigh, gazed up at him and permitted herself a small, slightly smug smile. She'd done it. She'd tamed the mighty beast of the corporate boardroom.

She lazed with this thought for all of five seconds before his silver-blue eyes popped open.

"Why do you hate Bethany?"

Ruefully, Edie wondered which of them really had been tamed. "I don't hate her."

"No?" He sat up and drew her next to him, one capable hand making lazy circles on her backside. "Then why are you always sniping at each other?"

Danger, Will Robinson. Telling Everett about Aurora and Leadbottom was revealing; explaining Bethany would strip bare her childhood. She opened her mouth to give him a comfortable lie.

Knocked clean out of her head when he smiled at her, unleashing the dimple.

Stealth dimple. That sucker was dangerous. She jumped up, found her scattered clothes. The silence stretched while she put them on. She turned to tell him but nothing came out. Even dressed, she didn't feel any less exposed.

He stood, came and gathered her gently into his arms. "You don't have to."

Perversely, that decided her. She took a deep breath. "Bethany and I...we grew up in the same commune."

"I didn't know those still existed. You, I can see. But Bethany?"

"Sure, she proactively leverages the strategic paradigm now, but for the first part of her life she was as macrobiotic a little peacenik as I was."

"Huh." Everett urged her back onto the couch. She objected until he snagged her foot and started massaging. Objections turned into a little groan. "Go on," he said, as if his touch weren't making her relax into a puddle.

"Bethany's parents were originally Eighties yuppies. But when they joined us they were like born-again hippies, really vocal. First to shout over pollution, protest war, save the animal of the week. Wherever they went, they pushed Bethany out in front. She was practically a poster girl for us. Mmm, that feels nice."

"Bethany, a protest poster girl." His strong fingers soothed the ball of her foot. "The mind boggles."

"Eventually my grandparents pulled out of the commune so I could go to a good high school and college. Bethany and her folks were off on a crusade and I didn't get to say goodbye. I had trouble adjusting to public high school and by the time I wrote her, a few weeks had gone by. She didn't answer. I wrote several more times but she never got back to me."

"You didn't phone?"

"The commune had one emergency phone. We weren't supposed to tie it up with personal calls but I did eventually decide that not hearing from Bethany was an emergency. I got her parents. They told me she never wanted to speak with me again. I was shocked, and by that time we were into semester finals and, well, I'm not proud of it, but I lost touch with Bethany. You can imagine my surprise when I met up with her at HHE. I tried to talk to her about our past but she shut me out. She was very different. Maybe Howell changed her."

"Why would you think Howell did it? Because they're sleeping together?"

"It's a bit more. Working late one night I heard them arguing—loudly. Howell accused Bethany of being tawdry like her parents. She was shouting about her corporate worth. But she was crying too. Sobbing that she was just trying to please him." Edie pulled her foot from Everett's hands, tucked both feet under her. "I don't understand how she could do that, change to please a man. Speaking of, quid pro quo, Everett. Why do you hate Howell?"

"Hmm? Oh, I don't hate him." He tucked the blanket around her. "But someone is trying to push me out of my job. It's most likely Howell."

"You're kidding."

"I wish I were." He rose and started cleaning the table. "It was subtle until lately. Rumors about apparent indiscretions. Vague accusations of not being a company man."

"Covering for employees who won't toe the line?" Edie bit her lip.

"Nothing I couldn't handle." Everett bestowed a quick smile on her as he walked the papers to the trash. "But just before I left, false quarterly figures were forwarded to the board of directors. That was his mistake. If I can find out where those figures came from, I've got him."

"Are you certain it's Howell?"

"Who else? But I need proof." He cocked his head, staring thoughtfully at the dead phone on the stack of milk crates.

"More corporate Tarzaning?"

"Tarzaning." He picked up the phone base, turning it thoughtfully in his hands. "Is that a word?"

"It is now. What are you doing?"

"Even if the line gets fixed..." He shook the base. It rattled, like bits were loose inside. "We're not getting a call out."

Just when she was feeling a connection. "Poor Ms. Dooley, alone in the office, waiting for your call."

"She guards my back, Edie." It was a gentle reprimand.

"Yeah, sorry. You've convinced me that businesses are more dangerous than I thought."

He set down the phone, came and gathered her into his arms. "Don't worry. I can handle it." He kissed her nose.

At that moment, the delicious scent of cooking meat rose to tease her. "You know, Everett, I believe you can."

Chapter Twelve

To: ED@mythicmail.com
From: ThePrez@serenityrangers.com
Subject: Re: Are you a mind-reader?

Dear ED,
Thank you for understanding. You're beyond a mind-reader. You're a best friend.
I just wish mind-reading could nail down my enemy.
—Prez

Tarzaning. As Edie minced dried onion for the abbreviated stew, she pictured Everett clad in a loincloth and tie, swinging on a vine over the big main conference room table at HHE, overwhelming all opposition.

For a brief moment, in her imagination, she swung tight in his arm with him, protected from dangers below by his strength.

She sighed.

Everett Kirk had proved to be a man of hidden talents, and not just his survival skills. Deeply hidden were compassion and championship of the little guy. He wasn't the corporate ogre she'd thought.

She glanced at him. Flannel shirt, just like her. She wondered if, on the battleground between nurturing employees and exploiting them, he was really much nearer her side. Had her own extreme attitude polarized him into opposing her?

Edie set down her knife. The mental black-and-white map labeled "Us" and "Them" morphed into color. The board, Howells, Bethany, herself, Jack, clients, vendors, customers... Everett was caught in the middle of them all.

How difficult it must be to please everyone. How challenging to keep the whole company running smoothly and still maintain his personal integrity. No wonder he had headaches.

As she cooked, her eyes kept wandering toward him. He was knotting together more of his snares, the ones she'd mocked, the ones that had worked. His hands were competent and sure. She wanted them on her again.

He looked up, caught her watching him, and smiled. "Thanks for making lunch."

"By the time it's ready, it'll be more like dinner."

"I'm in no hurry." He sauntered over, and pulled her into his arms, hugged her close. He smoothed her hair. "I have to split firewood and lay the snares."

"Don't go too far."

"Why Edie, my fireball." His lips were warm on her neck. "I didn't know you cared."

She cared, more than was good for her. So much so that she was thinking how nice it would be to come home every day to this.

When he left to cut wood, her neck was still tingling.

Her stew was bubbling and she was washing some of her clothes in the sink when he returned.

"Look out for the line." She'd strung a makeshift clothesline between upper cabinet handles. "I'll do your clothes too, if you want," she called to him as he stripped off his outer garments.

"Thanks." Everett came and gave her a quick hug. Definitely habit-forming. He brought out a pile of clothes and laid it on the counter as she rinsed hers. He gave her a sweet kiss, then took a sopping shirt from the sink and wrung it out with his hands. He hung it on her line, straightening it to dry better.

"You do that almost as if you know what you're doing. Your mother?"

"Serenity Rangers International, actually. That, and many years of bachelorhood."

"I thought you'd have a cleaning service." Actually, she thought he'd have a succession of live-in roommates to handle domestic chores. She piled her wet laundry in the bucket then refilled the sink, adding soap and his clothes.

He kissed her hair. "Thank you."

"For dinner? Or laundry?" Her eyes closed as he stood behind her and hugged her, her hands going still in the wash water.

"You could have blamed all this on me. Instead, you've done everything you can to make our stay here pleasant." He kissed her cheek.

Her eyes opened. "It was my fault too."

"Let's not argue about that. In fact, let's not argue about anything." His mouth found hers and she turned from the wash into his arms. It felt good, right.

It felt like the first day of the rest of her life. A life that included him.

But stupid company policy...

Everett's competent hands worked their way down her backside, and she forgot all about company policy.

*

That evening, full of rabbit stew, Edie decided she wanted a bath.

"I don't think that's such a good idea," Everett said. "The tap water isn't much warmer than melted snow."

"I'll add boiling." She hauled out a couple pots. "You did it."

"I needed a bath. You don't."

"On the contrary. I reek worse than the rabbit cleanings." She filled the pots with water and set them on the stove.

"Please, Edie. You won't like it."

"Why, Everett. Finally admitting you took a cold bath?"

"No." He paused. "Maybe a little cool. I'll stoke the fire. I don't want you to catch a cold."

"How considerate. Does HHE suspect?"

"That I'm not a blood-thirsty savage in a tie? No, they'd fire me in an instant." He opened the stove and added wood. By the time she dumped the boiling water into the white claw-footed tub, the cabin felt like a sauna.

Everett tested the water. "I'll put more wood in the stove."

"Everett, if it gets any hotter in here I'll think I've been sent downstairs for my corporate sins."

"Hell?"

"Accounting."

"I don't want you to catch cold," he repeated stubbornly, and he left the room.

As Edie stripped, she heard the scrape of the grating and the thunk of wood. If it got any hotter, the cabin would spontaneously combust.

Then she eased into the cool water and goose bumps immediately ran up her flesh. When she sluiced water onto her head, the heat of her own scalp radiated through the river of cold. Her nipples were tight as lug nuts, and though she'd rather stuff a thumb drive up her bottom than admit Everett was right, the quicker this bath was done, the better.

She lathered and soaped frenetically. She had just dunked into the slightly brown, soapy water when Everett opened the door. "I'll do your back."

"Oh, would you?" She drew up her knees and smiled brightly at him, thinking *go away* so she could get out of this liquid ice cube and be warm. True, he'd seen all the parts before, but that was when he was blinded by lust. At this moment, he was unfortunately clear-sighted.

He rolled up his sleeves, grabbed a washcloth and soaped it. She leaned forward. He ran the cloth over her back, and she forgot all about being cold, her goose bumps forming for another reason entirely.

He kissed her damp shoulder.

Edie shivered. The cloth scrubbed rhythmically up and down her back. Her eyes closed. Up and down the washcloth went, up and down and then up and over...

And then he was washing her front and her arms were falling away. His indrawn breath let her know she was exposed to him.

"You're so beautiful," he whispered reverently.

Her eyes flew open. His gaze was blazing on her breasts, her belly. The water lapping at her thighs no longer seemed cool at all.

The washcloth adored her, stroking over her breasts, her tight nipples, caressing her skin. She wondered if he would kiss her, then decided what the heck, grabbed his head and kissed him instead.

He groaned, washing her harder, lapping her breasts and belly and between her tender thighs until she ached for him. Until her fingers were knotted in his hair and she'd tried to crawl down his throat with her kiss.

Until he dropped the washcloth and scrubbed her directly with his fingers, over and over until she lit up like the sun, shouting her climax.

Languid after, she murmured, "Would the company approve?"

"Who the hell cares?" Everett lifted her, streaming water, from the tub. He held her tightly against him, soaking his clothes. "I laid a blanket in front of the stove." Red patches flagged his cheeks. "To dry you off. Not for—"

"To dry *us* off." She smiled into his fever-bright eyes. "You're wet now, too."

With a growl he carried her naked to the main room, settled her on blankets spread before the wood burner.

He'd opened the stove's doors and put in the grate. It was hotter than hot. Edie shivered as lush heat skittered across her skin.

He knelt over her. Their eyes met and held and the heat seared through her veins.

Bending, he kissed down her jaw and neck. His mouth opened and he tongued the notch at her throat, nibbled the tender flesh of her breast. With a sudden growl, he fastened onto her nipple and tugged.

She panted his name. "You. Let me see you." She tugged at his damp shirt, eager to expose—everything.

"Edie, you'll rip it." Cuffs already open, he grabbed the hems of both shirt and sweater and pulled them over his head. Edie gazed reverently at the torso revealed. Powerful packed belly, heavily muscled chest, all covered by smooth skin and a sprinkling of chestnut hair—and, picked out on one pectoral by the flickering firelight, the faint echo of a tattoo masked by tiny silver scars.

"What's this?" She traced the scars with one finger.

His nipples tightened. "Nothing."

a"That feels good."

She grabbed his hair and yanked him down onto the blanket beside her. To be fair, he let her. "Where did you get it?"

"A misspent youth."

"Like the lock picks?" She straddled his hips and fumbled with his buckle.

"You'll leave the belt alone, if you know what's good for you." He raised himself on bent arms. His rapidly rising and falling six-pack and the growing bulge under her belied his words.

"Can't." She managed the prong and opened the buckle. Started to work on the pants. "Where did you get the tattoo?" He didn't answer. Bending, she tongue-tickled the short hairs on his belly. "Where?" She peeked up.

His eyes were glazed. "I ran...I ran with a wild group for a while."

"What group?" She licked his navel. Delicately inserted the tip of her tongue.

"*Dogs.*" The word sounded wrung from him. "The Street Dogs."

"You ran with a punk band? Scary." She peeked again.

"No," he laughed. "My neighborhood gang."

Suddenly he sat up, red flags on his cheeks. "It was long ago. My hitch with SRI straightened me out."

In intimate contact with his body, Edie noticed the stiffness in him immediately, and it wasn't the good kind. "Everett, what's wrong?"

"Edie, if Howell ever heard of this..." He gently dislodged her. "You're cold. Put on my robe. It's on the couch."

He slipped out from beneath her and disappeared into the bedroom, leaving her naked, overheated, and bewildered in front of the stove.

Chapter Thirteen

To: ThePrez@serenityrangers.com
From: ED@mythicmail.com
Subject: Please be careful

Dear Prez,
The person trying to force you out—why? What's his or her motive? That can give you a clue as to who it is. Does someone want your job? Or does someone hate you so much they're trying to ruin you?
If it's the second, watch out. That sort of person will stab you in the back.
—ED

Everett paced the bedroom. He'd handed her a fatal tool—and through her, maybe handed it to his enemy. If she told Howell about his gang connection…damn it, it wouldn't even be betrayal. Just telling the truth.

Edie was his precious fireball. But as much as he liked her and desired her and perhaps felt something more, he could only trust her to be herself. She was honest, forthright, and had every reason to hang him. He was the man who stood between her and her idea of good management. If not for him to draw on the management reins, she would be a happy wild filly.

Wild. Her face, reddened by the glow of the stove, as he'd pleasured her… He reached into his pants and adjusted things that wouldn't adjust. It would be a long evening.

Speaking of long evenings…she was out there with little to do but stew. Not a good way to leave things.

He sucked up his courage and braved the main room.

She was staring intently at the broken phone, wrapped in his kimono, the masculine garment entirely feminine when pulled snug around her sweet little body. He shifted stance. Next time he was buying baggier pants. "What are you doing?"

"I'm not sure." Her face was flushed, her curls unrulier than usual. Had he raked them with his fingers that they looked so adorably mussed? "I'm missing something, to do with this phone."

Suddenly he had to know. With anyone else he'd play the corporate game, dangle bait or lay a trap. But with Edie... He was constantly fighting the desire to bury himself in her, fighting the need to open himself to her. All subtlety abandoned him. "If it worked... Would you call the office? Would you tell them?"

Her brows furrowed. "About being stranded? Sure."

In another person that would be fencing, making him admit his fumble, emphasizing his precarious position. Edie truly didn't know. "About my gang connections. Management wouldn't be pleased." What the hell. The damage was already done. He was just assessing its depth. "Edie. You could have me fired."

Instead of reassuring him with fake promises or heartfelt lies, she only blinked at him.

His headache returned. He couldn't do this after all. He gathered the blankets from the floor and remade the couch. "Do you want the bed?"

"No." She was staring at that damned phone, not even realizing he was upset. "It's your turn."

"Of course. Good night, then."

"Good night."

When he left for the bedroom, she was still lost in thought.

*

Edie stared at the phone. Everett's words had startled her, especially when she understood what he was really asking. If the phone worked, would she betray him?

Never.

Except…it might be for his own good. He was courteous, sensitive, and idealistic. Leaving HHE could be a release for him.

It'd be, not betrayal, but freedom. He'd be free to be—with her.

A thrill sang through her. Everett, tethered to the corporate rules, was sexy and capable. How much more could he be if he could kiss and touch her freely, without restriction? She nearly ran after him to find out. To tell him how she really felt. She actually took a couple steps toward the bedroom.

But while she was sure Everett the untamed mountain man liked her, she wasn't so sure about the corporate hunter Mr. Kirk. Mr. Kirk might see her emotions as a weakness to be exploited.

Mr. Kirk could hurt her badly.

She stopped.

Everett's secret could kill off Mr. Kirk.

She sucked in a breath. Without Kirk, Everett would be the wonderful man she'd uncovered here in this cabin.

And all hers.

All she had to do was kill off the corporate predator.

*

Edie woke Tuesday morning to an empty cabin again. But her big wool gloves were gone, so at least he'd dressed warmly this time.

After washing the dishes and folding the dried clothes, she spent an hour picturing what she'd do to Everett when he returned, beginning at his toes and working her way up. But after a brief sojourn in the bedroom she was bored.

So she got out her old laptop and started playing with a little open-source database engine, finally get around to creating her Christmas card list.

The communications icon caught her eye.

Too bad there was no wireless here. She'd even take a working phone line. Assuming she remembered how to use dial-up. Jack had given her the number for the HHE server, but it was so long ago…

Her heart beat faster, her body catching the implications a split second before her brain did.

The phone didn't work. *But the line might.*

Edie leaped to her feet, laptop in hand. Her old clunker had a modem card. She ran to the phone, popped the connector tab and yanked the line out of the base, then plugged the connector into the computer. It made a small snick.

Crossing her fingers, she activated the dial-up program.

The beep-boop of her modem exploded in the still room. She pumped air. A live line! Now, if only she could connect.

The line went silent. She sat cross-legged and settled the laptop on her knees. Still no sound. The floor chilled her buttocks. Silent, too long.

The sudden hiss of a computer handshake jarred her taut nerves. A single beep and text reeled across her screen, a greeting and login prompt.

She grinned. "I'm in."

Her grin faded. If she was going to "free" Everett, best to do it while he was out of the cabin.

While he couldn't stop her.

Okay, good. Everett would be free, might even thank her. She got on the virtual private network, linked to her work desktop computer, and typed an email to Howell Senior.

Her fingers slowed. Stopped.

Everett would lose his job, like she'd lost hers at Broad Vistas. That had hurt. The weeks until she'd found another job had been scary. The nights worrying, the days dodging collectors' phone calls… Everett wouldn't thank her.

Blinking at the email, she remembered Philip betraying her. She clamped her eyes shut as realization struck her.

She wasn't freeing Everett.

She was punishing *Everett because of Philip.*

It horrified her. Her eyes popped open. She needed time to think. She canceled the email.

Immediately she felt relieved.

Okay, right decision. What next? Oh yeah, rescue. She switched from email to chat, and pinged Jack.

The chat window halved. Jack's bright, "Hey, Edie, how's sunny Californ-I-A :)" glowed on the bottom.

Edie typed in, "I'm caught in snowy UTAH!" and waited.

"You and the PRES?? Ooh-la-la!"

"Perv." It took Edie three times to type that, her hands were shaking so badly. "We're lost somewhere off I-70. Call the police. Trace this line and rescue us."

Nothing more was added to the screen and Edie thought she'd lost the line. But then the bottom half cleared and Jack typed, "Are you kidding me?"

Edie typed, "NO!!"

Chapter Fourteen

To: ED@mythicmail.com
From: ThePrez@serenityrangers.com
Subject: Meet?

Sorry for the long time between messages. I was tied up on business.

No, that's a little corporate white lie. No lies between us.

I spent a long weekend with her.

ED, I don't know what to do. You're maybe my best friend—but she's so damned exciting. I think about her all the time, even as I'm writing this to you.

This has got to stop. Can we meet? I'm sure that once I see you, this insane infatuation with *her* will go away.

—Prez

After they were rescued, Edie spent fifteen minutes with a doctor—and four hours with the company's lawyers and their paperwork. Not until four that afternoon did she unlock the new door of her apartment, dropping exhausted into bed despite the early hour.

The one time during the whole legal ordeal that she'd seen Everett, she'd smiled with relief and jumped up to talk to him—only to have him nod curtly and walk away.

She tossed and turned for hours before being thankfully roused by her grandparents who wanted a blow-by-blow description of her ordeal.

Blow. One of the things she and Everett hadn't fully explored. Maybe later...

But there would be no later.

She didn't sleep well.

The next morning when she walked into the office, she wasn't in the best of moods. Her heart ached, missing her mountain man lover. Oh, she'd see him here at HHE, but if yesterday were any indication, he'd be Mr. Kirk, not her Everett.

"Her" Everett, right. Not Everett, and especially not hers.

She shuffled by Jack's cubicle. Kirk the corporate animal had returned, the bastion of the good-old-boys... Bethany was perched on Jack's desk, legs crossed, rump round in her tight skirt. Edie shuffled by. Kirk, the ever-vigilant for WASP rights, Kirk the—what the heck?

Edie reversed. Nope, there was Bethany, hem pulled so high the lace of her thigh-highs showed, perched on Jack's desk. Yuck.

And Jack...double yuck with a dollop of ick. Jack was staring all moon-eyed at La B.

Edie braced fists on hips. "What's going on here?"

Jack jumped. "Edie! You're back." He smoothed his tie and pretended he hadn't gone all middle-school crush. "I thought you'd be at your management camp."

"Kirk is transferring my dates. And?"

"Well." He cleared his throat. "You were gone, and Bethany was my contact and, well, I asked her to help me out."

"Help you out." Edie narrowed her eyes. "With work?"

"That...and the raise I was supposed to get." He played with his tie. "It's been over a year."

Now it was Edie's turn to be embarrassed. "I've filed protests with management—"

"Bethany appealed directly to the top. In person. She got me scheduled for a special review."

Edie gritted her teeth. Sure, Bethany appealed "in person"— she slept with the COO.

And Edie had slept with the president.

No, she'd slept with *Everett*. And *she* wouldn't exploit that relationship. *She* had standards.

"Edie, there's Charlene and the kids I have to think of." Jack's eyes rounded in appeal. "I need that money."

A needle of shame popped Edie's self-righteousness. Her pride was not more important than her employees. If Bethany could get Jack a raise, then good for her. Edie cleared her throat. "That's great news, Jack. Congratulations, Bethany." She held out her hand.

Bethany's expression morphed from smug to stunned to furious. She hopped off the desk and struck Edie's hand away. "When you call me 'bitch' behind my back?"

Edie's cheeks heated. Apparently Jack had been talking about more than the job.

"You think you're so great, so much better than me. Fair warning, Edie. Houghton will be running this company soon, and you'll be out. And I, for one, will be glad to see the last of your self-righteous ass!" Bethany swiveled out.

"Nice exit." Edie sighed.

Jack had the grace to look slightly ashamed. "I wish you two didn't fight like that."

"We do seem to go right to DEFCON 1. Maybe she thinks she's in danger of losing her position as lead mare."

"Huh?"

"Never mind. Congratulations on your upcoming raise, Jack."

In her cubicle, Edie brooded. The incident knocked her already shaky composure. Bethany's sucking up had gotten Jack his much-needed raise, where Edie's crusading had gotten zero, zilch, *nada*, bupkis, freaking nothing.

For herself she didn't care. But for her people… She took a deep breath. For the good of her team, she'd do it. She'd be friendly and cooperative with management. Suck up to them… no. Not sucking up, just good manners.

Okay. Done deal. She sat in her cube and waited for her team to visit and notice how open-minded she'd become. Or Bethany or Howell, so she could practice being cooperative and friendly.

Or Everett...she looked up hopefully.

No one was there.

Days passed. Edie sat in her cubicle, trying to work but mostly fretting. No one visited to ask questions, look for direction, try for a kiss... Well, she'd been through a life-threatening experience and he—they were giving her healing space.

Unless he—they just didn't care anymore.

By Friday, she'd come up with and discarded half a dozen excuses to see Everett. Had he rescheduled her management camp—and would he like to discuss it over lunch? Were the new employee rules finished yet—and would he like to come to her apartment to show them to her? Each excuse seemed so transparent.

Saturday she even came in to the office, but no Everett wandered by.

By Sunday, she was desperate. The best of her batch of reasons was Jack's raise. Who would give Jack his special review? As Jack's supervisor, she needed to know.

Thus armed, Monday morning Edie sailed into the executive wing, right past Everett's inimitable guard, Ms. Dooley.

Straight into Houghton Howell III, feet propped on the corner of Everett's desk. Bethany sat nearby.

Edie marched into the office, slapped hands on hips and opened her mouth to shout: *What the hell is going on?*

Barely in time she remembered her resolution to be cooperative and friendly. "Comfy, aren't we?"

Howell smiled, his teeth like a wolf's. "Edie, how pleasant to see you. Unfortunately, we will only see you a short time. Kirk can't rescue you now."

Resolution evaporated. "What the *hell* do you mean?"

"Language, Edie." Bethany slid off the desk, sauntered to the door and shut it. "You didn't think even Kirk could cover up those profit and loss figures you manufactured, did you?"

"Manufactured figures?" Edie's anger faded into confusion. "What are you talking about?"

"Don't play innocent," Howell said. "You know exactly what figures. The faked fourth quarter profit-loss reports, conveniently leaked just before you disappeared. The board of directors is not happy. And when the board is unhappy, management must act."

Edie glanced from Howell to Bethany and back, disliking their twin smug expressions. "I don't do financial reporting."

"The VP of Finance put the files online before leaving on vacation. Kirk forecast a profit but these numbers show a nasty loss."

"In Mr. Kirk's absence," Bethany said, "Ms. Dooley asked me to check them out. The report files are stamped with your username, Edie. *You.* And I traced the originals back to *your* computer."

"Only one set of figures is correct." Howell smirked. "If Kirk's are correct, you're out. Of course, Kirk is soft on you. He might pretend your numbers are correct—and commit political suicide."

Edie sucked in her breath.

Bethany smirked just like Howell. "Mr. Kirk's been protecting you for years, but not this time. You're history. I warned you."

Howell pulled a cigar out of his breast pocket and meticulously clipped the end. "I'll miss you, Rowan. Cleaning up after your uncooperative little butt made Kirk weak. I liked that."

"I didn't do it." Edie's blood drained out her feet, leaving her cold and shaken. "Whatever proof you think you've found. Where's Mr. Kirk? He'll straighten this out."

"Oh come now, my dear." Howell stuck the cigar in his mouth while Bethany lit it. He drew on it, blew out a lavish cloud of smoke. Heavy fumes filled the air. "I never thought you had the corporate savvy to try such a bold power play, taking out the president. I admit I was wrong."

"Please." Gritty smoke stung Edie's eyes. "Where's Mr. Kirk?"

"He won't save you this time," Bethany said gleefully.

"I don't need rescuing." But Edie felt stabbed to the heart. "Last time. *Where the hell is Everett?*"

"Right here, Edie."

She spun. The door had opened silently and Everett Kirk's big frame filled the doorway. Never had she been so glad to see him.

But something was off. Oh, his navy pinstripe suit and saffron tie were as imposing as ever. But his crisp white cotton shirt was just this side of wrinkled. And his voice sounded tired.

Her confidence wavered. Was he tired because of her? Did he believe Howell? Did he think she'd faked those numbers? Anger fired her. How could he ever think that she would betray him?

Except she *had* thought about betraying him, for his own good.

In the mirror of Everett's silver-blue eyes, she saw her own guilt. It scared her.

But what scared her worse was if he *did* believe her. He'd mount a rescue that would be corporate seppuku.

He swung casually into the room, as if none of this was on his mind at all. "Hello, Houghton, Bethany. Mind if I have my office back?"

"Not at all, my friend." Howell shot Everett a quick sly grin and stood. "For as long as it *is* yours. Come along now, Bethy, honey." He gave her fanny a little pat.

A grimace crossed Bethany's face. Howell threw an arm around her and steered her out.

Everett watched them leave, eyes narrow. After a moment he shut the door—and locked it with a click that skittered down Edie's spine. "We need to talk." He gestured at the guest chair, face stern.

She sank into the chair. "I didn't do it, Everett. I mean, Mr. Kirk."

She expected him to sit behind his desk, putting the Great Wall of China between them; the emotional chasm felt just as big.

He surprised her, sitting next to her in the other guest chair. "I know you didn't. But there's proof against you."

"What proof? The original files are on my computer? It's on the network. Anyone could have created those files while I was gone."

"They were in your private directory."

"Impossible." Edie gaped at him. Security on the system was tight. Her private directory was encrypted and password protected. Exactly one account could create files in her directory—hers. This was like finding the dead body in her locked bedroom, Edie herself standing over it with bloody knife in hand. "It would require my password."

He nodded. "You must have told someone."

He was giving her a way out. One she couldn't take. "Except I haven't."

"Someone guessed it then."

"No. My password is the name of my goldfish." Jean-Luc Picardfish had died three years ago, before she'd ever come to HHE. "No one here has ever heard of him."

"While I admire your honesty, that's bad news. Could someone have used brute force?"

Again she had to be honest. "No. There's a lockout after three attempts. All lockouts are logged."

"Rats." Everett heaved a breath. "I don't know what we're going to do this time. What I'm going to do."

"Everett…" All these years he'd protected her, cleaned up after her mistakes. The care and worry in his eyes told her it was true. She was ashamed of herself. "You don't have to do anything. This is my problem."

He smiled sadly. "I won't abandon you."

"Careers are at stake besides mine. Jack's, the rest of my team… Everett, they need you to survive." To show him she really meant that, she leaned in and kissed him.

She would have drawn away after a moment, but his hand slid behind her head and he pulled her onto his lap, drawing her into his strength.

And because she was really scared, she went gladly.

He hugged her close and she clung to him. He kissed her hair reassuringly, her forehead, her eyes, her cheeks.

Finally he lifted his head. "I was looking for you just now. I'd been pulling every string I knew to avoid this, but... A disciplinary meeting has been called for tomorrow. Executive managers." He kissed her lips once again. "Edie, my love, I'll do whatever I must to protect y—"

She put a finger to his lips, stopping him.

My love. It echoed in her heart, and opened her eyes to a very painful truth. Mr. Kirk hadn't abandoned her. Everett had been working nonstop to save her. But it wasn't enough. She was going down.

And more. To survive this fiasco himself, he'd have to distance himself from her.

The old Edie would have considered it betrayal.

Now she knew better.

She'd put her mentor Philip in the same position, demanding he choose sides between her and Leadbottom. With a wife and a mortgage, he'd done what he thought was right, rather than what Edie thought was right, and she'd felt betrayed. She'd forgiven him but had never really accepted his choice.

Yet with Everett, she not only accepted his choice, she embraced it. And in embracing it she accepted who Everett Kirk really was, rather than who she wanted him to be.

She released her death-grip on him, to stand on her own two feet. It felt as if she had aged decades overnight.

But she had to be her own corporate tiger for a change. She forced herself to the door. Turned and offered him a sad smile. "I'm a big girl now, Everett. I can protect myself."

He stood, his body powerful in suit and tie. "I'll do what I must," he repeated.

It wasn't the suit that made him strong, but the crystal clarity of his mind and the iron resolution of his will. He had covered for her all these years. Defended her. He was strong and brave.

How could she be any less?

Chapter Fifteen

To: ThePrez@serenityrangers.com
From: ED@mythicmail.com
Subject: Re: Meet?

Dearest Prez,

I'm sorry, I can't meet you. In fact, though it's shredding my heart, I have to say goodbye.

You're one of my truest friends, Prez. But I think I've fallen in love.

How strange that sounds. I don't even know if he and I have a future.

I have to be honest with you, though. This man is kind and funny and strong and…well, everything I need and want.

Good luck, Prez. I'll miss you.

—ED

She wanted what was best for Everett. Whether that meant she loved him or not, she wasn't going to stand by and let him take the fall for this in front of executive management.

She'd take the fall.

If there had been time to investigate, to straighten things out… but there wasn't. That was okay. She'd never fitted properly at HHE anyway.

Tuesday morning her heart was at peace when she took her seat at the big main conference room table.

Two mid-level managers guarded the door, security to escort her out. Across the table from her, like a row of hanging judges, sat HHE's senior officers. She knew them all but three stood out.

Houghton Howell the Copy grinned his barracuda best at one end. Howell the Original, eyes glittering in deep dark bags, anchored the other. Philip Sedgwick, back from his vacation, hunkered in the middle. Once she might have thought of him as the Knight but time and reality had tarnished his shining armor.

Besides, she was into loincloths these days.

At the head of the table was Everett, her corporate Tarzan. He looked tired but his jaw clenched in that determined way she recognized. Her heart was fiercely proud of him.

"Ladies and gentlemen, if we can get this special meeting started." Everett's voice was deep and sure. "We're here today to consider Ms. Rowan's part in the falsification of corporate figures."

Edie only half-heard him. In his midnight blue worsted suit, his crisp white shirt and his bold yellow tie, he was the handsomest man she'd ever seen, in the wild or not.

"I am hereby absolving Ms. Rowan of any blame in this affair."

Edie's jaw dropped.

Howell Junior shot to his feet. "It's been proven!"

"Kirk." Howell Senior fired a narrow look at Everett. "I thought this meeting was a mere formality. Now you say she's innocent?"

"Yes. I know Ms. Rowan. She couldn't have falsified those figures."

"How do you explain the files?" Junior rapped the table. "The directory was password protected. No one could have created them but—" He pointed dramatically. "Edie Rowan herself."

"Ms. Rowan is innocent, end of discussion." Everett rose. "Now, if there's no further business—"

"Wait a minute." Howell Senior's eyes gleamed in their dark pillows. "We convened to fire the perpetrator. If the Rowan woman is innocent—"

"You'll have to take the blame." Junior almost howled in triumph. "Kirk, you're fired!"

For just one moment, Howell Senior hesitated. Then he said, "Yes, quite."

"I'm sorry you feel that way." Everett straightened to his full height, as tall and proud as the day he'd trapped the rabbits. He pulled out a single sheet of bond, laid it on the table. "My resignation."

"Everett, no!" Edie blurted. Everett shot her a fierce look, part concern, part command, part naked longing. She hesitated for a critical half second.

Everett strode out.

With a flick of fingers, Howell Senior sent security scurrying after. Junior rushed off in the other direction, probably to squat in the president's office. The conference room emptied.

Edie, stunned, was left alone with Houghton Howell Senior.

"That was unfortunate," the elder Howell muttered.

"I beg your pardon?"

The old man sighed, met her eyes. His were no longer gleaming, but faded and sad. "Young Kirk is the best executive in the history of this company. Including me."

Edie stared at Everett's resignation letter, lying on the table. "Then why let him go?"

"I had to, my dear. It wouldn't do to appear weak, especially at my age." Pulling a cane from under the chair, Howell Senior rose unsteadily and shuffled out.

*

Everett was gone.

Edie tried to see it as a good thing. Maybe, outside of HHE, he'd revert to her beloved mountain man. With no more company policy and corporate espionage, maybe they could be together.

After the initial shock wore off, she called Everett's cell. It rolled immediately to voicemail. She left a message. An hour later, she left another. And another a half hour later. She kept trying all day, when the automated voice messaging system told her his mailbox was full.

She managed to get his home phone with a little judicious data diving, and tried that, chewing her fingernails. She got his answering machine. That one filled quickly too.

So she confronted Everett's faithful secretary, Ms. Dooley. It took three days of worried badgering before Ms. Dooley broke down and admitted that: "Mr. Kirk has retired to his summer house in the mountains." Or maybe she was that worried too. She gave Edie the address.

Saturday morning, before the sun was up, Edie drove to Utah. In the two weeks since the snowstorm, the roads had been plowed and treated with ice-melt, but her stomach churned as if they were still treacherous, and she clutched the steering wheel with white knuckles. Even with GPS, her nerves got her lost twice.

Finally she found the long private driveway of frozen dirt and ice. She rounded the last curve to a clearing, twice as beautiful as their lost cabin because Everett, stripped to his T-shirt despite the clear, cold day, was there splitting wood. She was so glad to see those broad shoulders twisting with exertion that she didn't even think to yell at him for doing such a dangerous thing alone. Well, for a couple seconds at least.

He finally looked up when she parked the car. She hopped out and ran to him, arms open wide—

His eyes were dead.

She stuttered to a halt. Her arms dropped. "Everett?"

"Hi."

"We need to talk."

"Okay." He put down his ax.

"Everett, you need to come back. Fight for your job. Howell Senior said you were the best…"

He turned from her mid-sentence to trudge into the cabin.

She ran after him into a rustic room with all the curtains drawn shut. "Everett, did you hear me? I talked to Howell Senior after that meeting, and he didn't really want to lose you—"

"Coffee?" Everett held out a battered metal pot that stank of burned dregs.

Dust mingled with the sting of coffee to make her sneeze. "Um, no thanks. Everett, about that meeting, I'm glad for what you did for me, but it really wasn't necessary because—"

"Have a seat." He waved vaguely at an old couch.

Edie blinked. Had he not heard her? "You can get your position back. You did nothing wrong."

"I'm sorry, did you say you wanted coffee?"

She stood in the doorway, completely at a loss. Her usual direct, in-your-face approach was failing abysmally. Everett was… not really here. Polite, but so very, very alone. Walled off.

"Well. Maybe this was a mistake." She shifted awkwardly. "But before I go, I want you to know…I think…well I'm pretty sure… Everett, I lo—"

"Okay." He turned from her to shuffle the coffee pot back to the stove.

A tear brimmed in Edie's eye. She dashed it away before it could fall. "Okay. I guess I'll be going. Unless…?"

She didn't know what she expected, a sudden declaration of need, a vow never to give up the good fight.

A return "I love you."

But he only set down the pot and shuffled back outside.

She shut the door behind her. As she went back to her car, she kept hoping…but he was absorbed in his work. She got in her car and started the engine, knowing she should do *something* but at a loss for what.

Her last sight was of him splitting wood. His shoulders were just as broad, his strokes just as sure. He was her mountain man, rugged and individual. The Everett she'd thought she wanted.

But he was no longer whole. A part of him had died—the part she'd thought she hated.

She went home. When she woke Sunday, her pillow was wet.

*

Monday at work, Edie got sucker punched walking past Everett's office. Howell Junior sat there, in Everett's chair, dictating to Everett's secretary. Bethany's promotion over Edie, announced later that day, and her move into a corner office was almost anticlimactic. Bethany finally had the vast real estate to go with her ego.

So it was a complete surprise when, at seven o'clock that evening, Bethany slipped into Edie's cubicle.

Edie was working late because she couldn't bear going home to another damp pillow. Ms. B'Promoted-itch was the last person she expected to see, or frankly wanted to.

But one look at the blonde's ashen face and red-rimmed eyes and Edie pushed away her keyboard. "Bethany, what's wrong?"

"You've got to promise not to tell anyone." Bethany ran a hand through her hair, messing its perfection. "I just don't know where else to go. Everyone here is such a corporate animal."

Laughable, coming from Bethany, but Edie didn't laugh. "It's okay, Bethany. I won't say a word. What's going on?"

Bethany dropped into the guest chair, twisted her hands in her lap. "It's Houghton. Someone's trying to get him fired. They're circulating nasty rumors. Like I got my promotion by sleeping with him."

"Rumors happen, Bethany. Ignore them."

"It's worse than usual. These rumors are *vicious*." She hiccupped, a suppressed sob.

Edie shuddered to think what sharkette Bethany might find vicious. "Can you be more specific?"

"When he was young, well, Houghton did some bad things." Bethany lost her battle with the tears. Mascara started running. "He's not so naive now. Why can't they see he's a better man, a better leader because he's learned from his mistakes?"

Bethany, in *her* cubicle, asking for her help to rescue *Junior*. Edie would've looked for webcams but Bethany wasn't acting—she'd never let her mascara streak. Edie pulled a tissue from her desk dispenser and offered it. "You're sure it's deliberate? Not just office gossip?"

"The timing, the people talking…" Bethany took the tissue and dabbed delicately at the mass of black, as effective as attacking burst toner with a cotton swab. "Yes, it's deliberate."

And if it was the same corporate killer who'd targeted Everett… it implied Howell hadn't been the one to ruin Everett. She'd have to let him know.

Except Everett didn't care. Her corporate Tarzan was gone, sacrificed for her.

She'd just have to deal with this herself for now.

She eyed Bethany thoughtfully. Maybe not totally by herself. "Pull yourself together, Bethany. Where is the girl who braved pepper spray to plant a protest sign in the mayor's front yard?"

Bethany colored. "That was a long time ago."

"You've changed, yes. But I can't believe you've lost your nerve."

The flush deepened. "No. But where Houghton is concerned I…I just don't want to screw up."

"If he's going to get fired," Edie countered, "how can you make that worse?"

A steely glint entered Bethany's raccoon eyes. "You're right."

"Darn right, I'm right. And what did my grandparents teach us?"

"Never give up." A beat. "But then they left." Bethany's tone cooled.

"I had college coming." Edie had heard bitterness in Bethany's voice but didn't understand it. "They thought school was important."

"My parents didn't."

"But you went anyway, didn't you? You couldn't be where you are today if you hadn't gone to college."

"Shit." Bethany stared at her. "You don't know. You really don't."

"Know what? Bethany, I tried to contact you—"

"When you left, my life went to hell." Bethany slumped. "You know why my parents joined the commune? Not the ideals, despite their public zeal. No, they wanted to grow 'medicinal' marijuana without getting jailed again. Those cross-country protest trips? A blind for selling drugs. After you left, my folks gave me a gift—my first tab of E. Ecstasy, for my fourteenth birthday."

"My God," Edie whispered.

"Without your grandparents there, my parents dropped any pretense of caring about me, left me to fend for myself. I got out of there."

"Your parents said you didn't want to talk to me. But you were gone. I...I never knew."

"No. You didn't." Bethany crushed the tissue in her hand. "I clawed my way up the ladder to financial security. I sold what I had to, to make it through school, did what I had to, to enter the privileged world of corporate America. And I'm glad I did it, do you hear me? I'm glad!" She was trembling.

"I'm so sorry." Edie didn't know what else to say. Bethany's anger made sense now, and she had a right to it. "Nobody helped you? Not even Howell?"

Bethany was silent for so long Edie thought she hadn't heard. Then, in a voice Edie remembered from girlhood, Bethany said, "I love him." Black rivulets trickled quietly down her cheeks. "At home he's just the sweetest pussycat. But at work he...he's ashamed of me."

"Why do you say that?"

"My ideas...he cuts them down. Says they're stupid." She paused. "Just like my parents."

"Howell's wrong. Your parents were *wrong*." Briskly, Edie pulled out more tissue and handed it to her. "You're strong and brave, Bethany. You have ideas worthy of respect."

Bethany looked away. "No one respects me."

"Everett does. He respects all the employees." Edie made a face. "Even me."

"He's got a thing for you." Some of the old acid Bethany cut through.

"And I thought you were the one in bed with him." Edie's whole face burned. "Corporately speaking."

"Hardly." Bethany dabbed her eyes. "Mr. Kirk is out of my league. You only have to look at him to see he's special."

Everett's protective coloration. He'd let Edie see through it to the real man. Half of whom she'd rejected. Her eyes suddenly prickled. She grabbed her own tissue.

Bethany shook her head. "Even Houghton feels intimidated by Mr. Kirk."

Such incredible personal power that he intimidated Mahogany Row just by breathing — yet he respected the employees. Respected her. At that moment, in Edie's mind, Edward Everett Kirk rose to a place just a little higher than her beloved grandparents.

She stood. "Bethany, I think whoever is sabotaging Howell got rid of Everett. We need to do something about this corporate killer."

"Us? You and me?" Bethany just stared at her. "We have no power. We aren't even officers. What can we do?"

"Together? What *can't* we do?" Edie hooked an arm with Bethany and tugged her to her feet. "We will overcome."

Chapter Sixteen

To: ED@mythicmail.com
From: ThePrez@serenityrangers.com
Subject: Re: Re: Meet?

Dearest ED,

Thank you for your honesty. Now it's my turn to be honest with you—and myself.

I've been playing the corporate game too long. It has lost me friends and made me enemies. And now, this stupid pointless game has cost the woman I love.

Time for me to make my own game.

Make your own game, ED. Grab that stupid man and shake him until his bones rattle if you love him.

Make your own game, ED. It'll be the best in town.

I won't be writing any more either. It was good knowing you. The best.

—Prez

"What the hell is that singing?" An irritated tenor presaged the appearance of Houghton Howell III.

"Houghie!" Bethany flung herself into his pinstripe-clad arms.

He caught her, hugged her briefly, and then held her at arm's length with a grimace. "Please, Ms. Blondelle, not in the office. Especially not in front of the staff."

Bethany drew herself up with dignity. "It's after hours, Houghie."

Edie, thanks to Everett, was too mature to stick out her tongue. But she thought "gotcha." "Don't mind me, Howell. I'm not the one killing your career."

That got his attention. "What do *you* know about it?"

"Only what I've heard from Everett, and now Bethany."

"What does Everett have to do with anything?"

"Come on, Howell. You think he got canned because your dad was anxious to sit your butt in his chair?"

Howell frowned. "I was just glad to see him go."

"Open your eyes. Somebody helped Everett out the door. It wasn't Bethany. Apparently it wasn't you."

"Me? Hardly. Everybody knows you were the one always harassing the poor man. Those faked reports were just the killing blow."

"I didn't fake them." Edie stared into Howell's eyes, trying to discover his real face behind the corporate mask. Everett had one, but she still wasn't sure about Junior. "Believe me."

"Why should I?"

Smack him with a clue bat. "Because we need to work together if we're going to discover who's really behind this. To do that we need to trust each other."

"Trust you? No way." Howell stalked off.

"Houghie, she can help." Bethany ran after. "Please, Houghie? For me?"

Howell turned, his narrow face astonishingly soft. "All right. For you."

Bethany touched his arm, smiling up into his eyes.

Edie looked away. Couldn't always choose your allies. At least she *had* allies. "So, we're in this together. I have an idea to find out who planted the fake files in my directory, but I'll need root privilege."

"Root?" Bethany said. "But only the vice president of MIS has root privilege."

"And the officers of the company." Edie stared directly at Howell.

Howell's eyes met Edie's, a feral gleam in them. "Ms. Rowan. If it catches this scum, I'll be glad to help."

*

The next evening, Edie waited for the last person to leave. Jack did the all call at 1 a.m., then keyed on the alarm system. The moment he left she keyed it off. Couldn't have the motion detectors betray her. She'd erase her electronic tracks later. Corporate politics, she'd learned, required a mild touch of paranoia.

Then she slipped into Howell's office and cracked her knuckles. Time to show who was alpha geek.

She called up remote desktop to log onto her own computer. A directory command on her private directory confirmed the fake profit/loss files were there, owner Rowan. Just for grins and giggles, she tried opening one. As Howell had said, password protected. Losing the grins, she tried her password, the name of her deceased goldfish.

The file opened.

"*Shi*...atsu massage." These fake files used her *real* password. How the *hel*...en of Troy had someone gotten her password? She never wrote it down, never told anyone. Had a rootkit or a computer virus trapped her keystrokes? But no, she used a virtual keyboard. A sledgehammer, guessing all combinations? No, there was a three-try limit until lockout, and the lockout report was clean.

She tapped her chin. Who knew about Jean-Luc Picardfish? She'd gotten him after leaving the commune, had him until just after she lost her first job. So her grandparents knew, and her high school and college friends. But no one *here*. Not Bethany, not Everett, not Howell, not even...

No. *He* was impossible.

She needed more information. She added flags to the directory command to view more information. The expanded list scrolled onto the screen. Date created was the Friday before the snowstorm, the time 7 p.m., well after she'd gone home. But he'd just argue that she'd netted in from home. Creator…Rowan. Either he'd actually logged in as her, or he'd managed to spoof all the attributes.

Okay. Everett had taught her that if she couldn't see the enemy in person, maybe she could find his spoor.

Friday night. Wouldn't be a lot of people working. How many computers were active? She got a break—only two IP addresses. One was Jack's, accessing a video on the Internet.

The other, located in the small conference room, was netting to her computer. "Gotcha."

She cross-referenced with the security cams, found camera fourteen covered the small conference room. She clicked to select the camera and started playback from Friday at 7 p.m.—

"*Damn.*"

There, typing away, was the man responsible for the evil rumors undermining Everett, then Howell. The man who knew her password, because he'd known her three years ago. The savage corporate animal.

Philip Sedgwick. Her mentor.

*

Edie had to get out of there. She triggered her cleanup routine, which ghosted an image of an empty office into the security footage, erased all traces of herself in the logs, set the building alarm to do an activation after five minutes, erased itself from the log, and shut down.

She grabbed her coat and purse, and ran out of the building.

But she was too worked up to drive. Pacing the parking lot, she tried to figure out what the H-E-rats-rats to do. She wasn't dressed for the cold but was too angry to care. She wanted to strangle Philip for betraying her a second time. She wanted to murder him for destroying the man she was coming to love, just as she finally took off her blinders and recognized that love.

When she calmed down it was 2 a.m. and she was bone tired and freezing. She got in her car and drove home.

As she neared her door, she heard her landline ringing. She was still clumsy with the new key and fumbled with the lock several seconds before it opened. When she ran inside the answering machine had already picked up and the tone sounded.

"Where the hell are you?" Everett's baritone barked.

She dropped her purse and ran to the counter, nearly squirted the handset onto the ceiling trying to pick the call up. "Don't swear." She was panting.

"Edie, thank God. Where have you been?"

Discovering Philip The Rat was a character murderer. But if she told Everett that, he'd swing in on his vine, straight into the spears of an enemy who'd already taken him out...she shivered. No, Philip had done enough damage. "Out."

"Out where?"

Commander Kirk was apparently up and taking nourishment again. But she was not going to risk him in the front lines. She hardened her heart. "What do you want, Everett?"

"To make sure you were all right. I heard something—"

"You knew I was all right when I visited."

"I wasn't myself then." He paused, seemed thrown by her coolness. "No matter how much you're prepared for it, getting fired is a shock."

So is finding out your mentor framed you. "You resigned."

"Officially. But emotionally, I was fired. Edie, I'm sorry. I know it was a shock for you too—"

"No, I'm fine. So if that's all—?"

"Edie, please." There was soft longing in his voice. A pause, and she knew he was about to speak the words that she'd yearned for, the words that would thaw her heart.

She couldn't afford that. Not and keep him at a safe distance, not yet. "Everett, it's late. I need to go."

"Are you okay—"

"I'm fine. Good night, Everett."

"Edie, I—"

She hung up. Then she lifted the handset and left it next to the base. The dial tone was colder than the snow outside.

Chapter Seventeen

"Sedgwick. The bastard." Bethany's heels flashed as she paced Everett's...Howell's office. "He's obviously after the presidency. We need to do something about him, fucking *now*."

"Language, Bethany." Edie sat in Everett's...*Howell's* guest chair. She hadn't even gotten through HHE's doors when Bethany dragged her, past two tall strangers in black suits and a very jumpy Ms. Dooley, directly into this meeting.

"I say we kill the bastard." Howell stabbed the desk with a finger.

"Please don't swear." Edie was uncomfortable with Junior's barely disguised corporate bloodlust. Everett, even in full suit-and-tie glory, was nothing like this. How could she have missed the obvious difference?

"Murder, I like." Bethany dumped herself into the other chair. "But think of the paperwork."

"No problem," Howell said. "It's all done on the computer now."

Bethany grimaced. "Whatever we decide, it has to be done today. We're out of time." She reached behind her to massage her nape.

"Why?" Edie asked. "What's the rush?"

Howell rose. "More profit-loss reports have surfaced. Annual." With an embarrassed glance at Edie, he moved behind Bethany and started massaging her shoulders.

Bethany startled, then melted into her chair. "That feels wonderful, honey pie." She smiled like syrup over her shoulder. He smiled like sugar lumps back.

Eew. Edie almost wished for the Duke of Drama and his consort Her Grand Bitchiness back. "Okay. Annual numbers. What's the problem?"

"They're not the real numbers, though I can't prove it," Howell said. "All indicators pointed to breaking even. But these reports show a horrible loss."

Edie rolled her eyes. "Again with the nasty rumors followed by faked reports. Sedgwick isn't too original, is he?"

"But he is effective. I got my hands on a draft hardcopy." He flipped open an orange folder on his desk. "These numbers are being leaked to both the board *and* the stockholders."

Edie leaned in for a look. Her eyes flew wide. "These won't destroy just *you*. Going to the stockholders? The stock will tank and the whole company will crash."

"Fortunately, no one else has seen the actual numbers, and I've been working my ass off plugging the rumors." Howell pressed small circles on Bethany's temples. "But it's only a matter of time."

"Mmm." Bethany said, "Which is why we need proof today. Daddy's called a special meeting of the board."

"So soon?" Edie said.

"Yes," Howell said. "You know those two guys in black suits and iron attitudes running around the company? Those aren't your average auditors. The Feds have heard about this, and falsifying business records is a felony. Now, normally they don't get involved unless investor cash or billions of dollars are at stake. But somehow HHE got in their crosshairs. They've already questioned Kirk, and, since I'm currently head of the company, they're gunning next for me."

Edie's heart skipped a beat. "The Feds have questioned Everett?"

"All that, and you're only worried about Kirk?" Howell shook his head. "He quit under suspicious circumstances. What did you think would happen? They questioned my father yesterday and I'm scheduled to get reamed this morning. I'm surprised they haven't pulled you in yet, Edie." He paused. "Say, I've got it. We show the board the security footage. That'll prove Sedgwick is the perp."

"That won't work," Edie said. "The camera shows Sedgwick typing, not *what* he's typing. Oh, God, why did the Feds question Everett and not me?" She leaped to her feet. "I've got to go. I've got to find evidence to clear Everett—"

"Sit down and stop worrying about Kirk. He hasn't been charged with anything yet, and he's walking free, isn't he? Worry about us. We're in the line of fire. Damn, I'm screwed. That fake loss makes me look like an incompetent leader. Worse, if we can't prove Sedgwick doctored the numbers, I look guilty. Edie. Isn't the IP thing proof that that Sedgwick planted bad files?"

Edie shook her head as she sat. "The board won't understand that. The Feds might, but it would take time to prove. In the meantime, it would be Sedgwick's word against mine, and who'd take the word of a computer geek against a vice president? You only believe me because Bethany trusts me, and you trust her."

"I have an idea, honey pie." Bethany turned in her chair to stare up at Howell. "Sedgwick's responsible for finance, right? Why don't you just tell the board and the Feds those awful numbers are his fault? They'll believe you."

"That," Howell said, "is the dumbest idea I have ever heard."

Bethany wilted.

"Why not?" Edie snapped. "I haven't heard anything better from you, Howell."

"Even if they believe me, Sedgwick's the guy who balances our books, not the one who decides our profit strategy. Hell, all he has to do is say he was following the orders of a superior officer—again, that's me—and I take the fall."

"Don't listen to the grump, Bethany," Edie said. "He's just jealous. You're at least coming up with possibilities. All he does is gripe and moan."

Bethany straightened. "You're not jealous of me, are you Houghie?"

"Me, jealous?" His tone held too much vehemence, too much

denial. He frowned, seeming to hear it, and sat slowly on the corner of his desk. "Bethy, I'm sorry. It's just… You're beautiful and smart. I'm just a mediocre businessman with an inheritance. I've seen *A Star is Born*. I know what happens."

"You really think I'm beautiful?" Bethany smiled like sugar lumps again.

Edie rolled her eyes. Out of all that, Bethany heard only beautiful?

"Of course, Honey Bunny." He smiled back, creamed goo.

To have something to *erk* in, Edie grabbed the orange folder. The reports distracted her. "This looks official. Sedgwick must have hacked the reporting software itself. Wait." She slapped the top page. "That means I can get the real figures and at least show Howell isn't incompetent."

"How?" Howell asked. "If he's rigged the report itself?"

She'd forgotten not everyone was as tech savvy as Bethany, or plain savvy as Everett. "I can bypass the report system and run a tabulation straight from the database."

He considered her. "You're as good as Kirk kept saying, aren't you?"

"Better."

"The real numbers…" Bethany snapped her fingers. "We can use the real numbers against Sedgwick. Make him explain why his are different. Use truth as a lever."

"Or a club." Howell grinned savagely. "That's brilliant, Bethy. Sedgwick is used to operating in the shadows. I'll back him into a corner, break his nerve. We won't need proof. He'll be bleating his guilt. Thank you, sweetheart." He took her hands in his. The sugar-honey-barfy lumps had come back in his eyes.

"You're so very welcome, Houghie." Her expression softened.

The atmosphere went toxically gooey again, so Edie left.

*

Edie did her data wrangling at 10 p.m. It went quickly and soon she was printing off the annual profit numbers directly from the accounting system. And the numbers did show a profit. Howell could confront Philip and force a confession from him. Although Philip would no doubt retaliate.

She stared at the printout. How like a game this corporate intrigue was, move and counter move. Philip floated rumors. Howell refuted them. Philip floated fake numbers. Howell brought in the real numbers. A game, or wolves in the wild, fighting for dominance. It might go on forever, the two of them tearing at each other's throats. Until one of them went down.

Like Everett had gone down, taking the killing bite meant for her.

Her throat thickened and her eyes itched. She stuffed the printout into her purse, wiped at her lids, and headed out.

Chapter Eighteen

The next morning Edie made copies of her printout for the board. Then she and Bethany followed Howell to the main conference room where the board—including Daddy Howell, Philip Sedgwick, and the two tall men whose black suits could have been tailored to cover shoulder holsters—were gathered. As Edie took her seat, Philip pointed an accusing finger at her. "What's *she* doing here? She's the one who got Kirk fired."

Edie's face heated. Philip was nasty but she was unprepared for that knife. Even his rusty armor fell away. He'd called it working behind the scenes but sometimes a person just stood up for what was right. And sometimes she just stood up for her friends.

"Gentlemen. Ladies." Thankfully, Howell took the attention from her. He walked around the table, sliding packets in front of each person. "These are profit and loss reports for the year, as produced by our VP of Finance, Philip Sedgwick. As you can see, there's apparent cause for alarm."

Edie watched Philip carefully, but he showed no sign of being flustered at this announcement, although one of the board members flipped open his packet and gasped. He obviously hadn't heard about the rumored loss of $10 million.

Capitalizing on the shocked silence, Howell sat across from Philip and rapped the glossy cherry finish in front of him. "Well, Sedgwick? Any explanation?"

"Me?" Philip waved over the report. "I'm not operations officer."

"This report came out under *your* auspices. It must've been sitting on your desk well before today. Why didn't you warn us of such a horrendous negative amount?"

Murmurs around the boardroom indicated agreement.

Philip shrugged. "That's not my job. It's yours."

Howell slapped the table and leaned into Philip Sedgwick's face. "But these aren't the *real* numbers, are they?"

Instead of a stuttered confession, Philip smiled slowly, as if it was Howell who had walked into the trap. Philip said, "Of course they're real. Why would you say they aren't?"

Howell flinched.

"I didn't want to alarm the board prematurely." Philip stood. "But as you can see, there is indeed cause for alarm. Due to the incompetence of our top management."

Howell said, "Kirk—"

"Not just Kirk. The management *team* of CEO and COO. A significant loss, and they're now trying to blame me."

Next to Edie, Bethany turned white. Edie put a hand on her arm and tried to salvage the situation. "Your figures are wrong," she said. "This loss is not what the accounting database shows."

"Oh?" Philip raised a brow at her. "You've been mucking about in the data, Edie?"

Her blood boiled. He'd neatly pinned her into being in the wrong, again. Fury almost drove her to blurt she hadn't changed anything. Honest, forthright—and implying she could have criminally altered the figures, exposing her throat to Philip, who was just waiting for her to blunder.

Bethany saved her. "Mr. Howell asked Ms. Rowan to extract the annual profit directly from the data."

Philip's grin turned feral. "Ladies and gentlemen, this only proves my point. Get rid of the cheating, lying deadwood. Remove Howell and his bedmates here." He waved at Edie and Bethany.

Edie glared.

Philip smiled nastily. "I mean bedmate only in the political sense, of course. But this disgrace has gone on long enough. I move to wipe the slate clean. Get rid of these three, and hand over the reins of HHE to more…capable hands." He opened his palms to the board.

There was a deathly silence. Edie's heart hammered as she waited for someone, anyone, to speak out against Philip's monstrous suggestion. The Feds sat like statues, but she could feel the weight of their stares.

Howell Senior feebly cleared his throat. "I don't…but if that's what the board wants." He didn't seem to be breathing well. "I move—"

The door banged open. Heads turned.

Edie felt the fierce masculine presence, practically heard the raw, primitive call of the savage beast. When she looked up it was with a smile.

Everett strode into the room.

*

Philip whirled. "You were fired, Kirk. Get out."

Everett ignored him. "Let me come to the point. I have discovered evidence of a crime against this company."

The silent men in black turned toward him. They were listening.

"*Your* crime, Kirk." Philip's face was red with barely controlled fury. "With your conspirator Howell."

Howell Senior held up one hand. "Sit, Sedgwick. Kirk. How did you get this new evidence? You left over a week ago."

"I've had access to it all along. But it only made sense after I put it together with information Ms. Rowan gave me while we were stranded."

"You see?" Philip slapped the table as he sat. "Kirk admits they're co-conspirators."

"I admit I have respect for Ms. Rowan's abilities," Everett said smoothly. "And so should you. You see, I thought the loss numbers were faked. Ms. Rowan's information pointed out an alternative.

Ms. Rowan, would you please show the board what you found?"

She'd given him an alternative? She didn't know where Everett was going with this and nearly said so. Stopped herself. No, she trusted him. She passed around her printout.

"Thank you. Ms. Rowan's numbers are taken directly from the general ledger. The bottom line shows a modest profit of $1 million. But Mr. Sedgwick's numbers show a loss of $10 million." He raised one brow at Philip. "Why is that, Mr. Sedgwick?"

Philip spluttered. "You can be sure that I'll look into it!"

"Thank you. But I already have."

"Delving into company files after you were fired? I'll have you arrested."

Whispers broke out, and the two Feds started to get to their feet.

"No, you won't." Everett didn't even raise his voice to quell all action. "Ladies, gentlemen, please note the difference between Ms. Rowan's total and Mr. Sedgwick's. $11 million. That number is significant. Care to tell us why, Mr. Sedgwick?"

"I can't imagine." Philip sneered. "Get it, imagine? Because that's all this is, imagination."

"Hardly." Everett slapped another paper on the table, directly in front of Howell Senior. "This is the history for a certain property, purchased six months ago by Philip Sedgwick—for $5.6 million. Not his primary residence, by the way. Paid in full."

"So I bought a second house." Philip glared at Everett. "You have no proof of anything wrong."

"No." Everett strolled around the perimeter of the room, loose-limbed, superbly unconcerned. "But Petra Sedgwick does. Six months ago, that same amount—$5.6 million—went missing from her accounts. She's sole owner of a very lucrative international boutique that designs and sells children's clothes, and an heiress besides. She ordered a full audit and her accountant discovered that in addition to the $5.6 million, $150,000 had been siphoned off monthly for the last three years. The total amount missing—$11 million. Strangely, before Petra could dig any farther and find the perpetrator, the money…reappeared."

"So you have nothing," Philip said. "Nothing but coincidence and innuendo."

"On the contrary. When I heard about Petra's missing money, I suggested to her that she instead hire an investigations firm to dig into Mr. Sedgwick's movements and finances for the last three years."

"Foul!" Philip's fisted his hands on the table as his nonchalance slipped. "Our family's money is none of your concern."

"Family money? Please. Don't you mean your wife's money? She's the billionaire, with an ironclad prenup. Her detectives discovered that Mr. Sedgwick has an illegitimate child. He's been paying support for the past three years and recently bought that house, in which to install his mistress and their child."

"You *liar*." Philip's face went an alarming shade of red.

Everett spun. "Am I?" He strode to the table and stabbed Philip's report. "The loss was meant to seem faked. But it's real. Because you embezzled $11 million from HHE to pay off the money you stole from you wife. Not very smart of you, stealing it in one chunk. Then you diverted blame onto management here, in a power play to grab the reins for yourself."

"Liar!"

"Names, Philip?" Everett gently shook his head. "Mr. Howell. I don't belong to this board anymore, so I can only suggest you restrict Mr. Sedgwick's access while you get a full audit of the books. Thank you for your time." He turned to go.

"One moment, Kirk." Howell Senior was blinking rapidly. "How did you figure this out?"

"Ms. Rowan told me a few weeks ago about a scandal at Sedgwick's previous company. Where there's smoke, there's usually fire. I dug into public records and found one house in Philip and

Petra's name. Then I found the second house in Sedgwick's name only, and I called Petra. When I told her what I had found, she was more than happy to supply her details. By the way, Sedgwick, you'll be hearing from her lawyers soon."

With that, Everett spun and swept out, Edie's Tarzan and shining knight all in one.

*

Faces around the table turned to Philip, expressions dark.

"I assure you, ladies and gentlemen..." Philip's voice cracked. He coughed, tried again. "This is a mistake."

Howell Junior's smile gleamed in his narrow face. "Oh, it's a mistake, all right. Yours. Did you really think you'd be able to step into the presidency of HHE with your sly rumors and backstabbing?" Howell used his words like a knife. "I've heard some rumors of my own, Sedgwick. Care to comment on who your mistress is? Remember how you got an employee pregnant at your last company, and then fired her? Did you know she sued the company and nearly bankrupted them?"

"Greedy bitch," Philip spat. "She wasn't satisfied with that money. Her baby's father had to pay her too."

Edie gasped, putting it together. "Philip...Aurora...you?"

"You can't prove anything." Philip's eyes gored Howell. "No one can ever prove who the father was. The Rowan woman stampeded over the tracks."

Edie paled.

Philip turned a smile, shark-like, on her. "Oh, yes, my dear, you were very effective in distracting management. They were so busy trying to deal with your self-righteous mayhem, they never had time to discover who was really to blame. But it wasn't me." He winked.

Edie wished she could disappear into the floor.

"And then you were hired here, where you could screw things up for Everett Kirk, that smug bastard. Which you did, so well." He laughed.

"You got me hired here, Philip." Edie blinked stinging eyes. "You did it."

"Years of waiting, but you were the thorn that finally felled the mighty Everett Kirk. Then it was only a matter of sweeping aside Junior." Philip smirked. "But it wasn't *me* that did it."

"That's enough, Sedgwick," Howell said. "It was you and we'll find proof. Or they will." He nodded at the men in black suits. "In the meantime I invite you to leave. Now."

The men rose and came around the table to stand, one on each side of Philip, waiting.

"You're history, Howell." Philip surged to his feet. "I'm the clever one. I've got all the right things, the right wife, the right home, the right—hey!"

Howell Junior leaped to his feet, steamed around the table, grabbed Philip by the arm and hustled him out the door. The Feds followed. As they walked out of the boardroom, Philip tried to wriggle back in but Junior slammed the door in Philip's face. Then he turned and slapped his hands together in a satisfied *done*.

"Bravo, Houghton," Howell Senior said. "Ladies and gentlemen, come to order. We need to discuss the damage that traitor has done."

Edie slipped out of her chair, out of the conference room.

She was horrified. Philip had gotten her a job here, not because she was a wonderful manager.

But because she was a total jerk.

Eyes burning, she turned the opposite direction from the retreating tall backs in black herding an unbowed Philip, and returned to her cubicle. There, she reached for the desk phone, but stopped herself. This was personal. Instead, she dug her cell phone from her purse.

She called Everett. Maybe he hadn't left the building yet. Maybe he was waiting for her somewhere. Maybe...

He picked up, and before she could say a word shouted, "Edith Ellen Rowan, what the hell did you think you were doing?"

"Rats, Everett. What the rats did I think I was doing. And hello to you too." She was inordinately comforted just hearing his voice.

"What the iguana did you think you were doing, I don't care! Why didn't you leave Philip Sedgwick to me? Dammit, Edie, that's why I quit when I did. I was trying to protect you."

He'd been trying to protect her? Edie blinked scratchy eyes. "I didn't do much. Howell did most of it. How did you know the backstabber was Philip?"

"Please." The old arrogance was back in full force. "Once I'd left the cesspool of corporate politics and cleared my head it was simple enough to figure out. COO is next in line for the presidency, certainly, but right after that is VP of Finance. Howell's nasty, but he's a vulture. He'd only prey on me after I was dead. Sedgwick is the praying mantis."

"They're female," Edie said.

A beat. "Praying mantises are female?"

"The cannibalistic ones are."

"Edie, it was just an analogy. And not the point. The point was, I was trying to keep you from being implicated in this mess." His voice hardened. "But there you were, in the center of all the trouble yet again."

Her body drained of blood. "Everett, I'm sorry."

"Sorry won't turn back time, Edie."

There was an awful silence.

She cleared her throat. "But Everett... now that Philip's gone..." She had called Everett for a reason, a reason she'd barely dared to think. Now after hearing his hard tone, it took all her courage to say it. "You could come back. You could be president again—"

"No. I am *never* coming back to HHE."

Her heart broke. She didn't blame him for not wanting to work there anymore, but she'd hoped...but no. He didn't want to return for her, either. "Oh. Of course." Shoulders slumping, she hung up.

Then she typed out a short letter of resignation. There was nothing here for *her* anymore either. Leaving the letter on Howell's desk, she gathered her few things and left HHE forever.

Chapter Nineteen

Everett, is that you? Because if it is—I love you.
—Edie

That evening she Skyped her grandparents to break it to them that she'd failed. She'd tried to strike a blow for the little guy. All she'd really done was make life intolerable for the true corporate paladin.

Everett.

"So I resigned," she said after she'd stuttered through all that had happened. "As I walked out, Bethany joined me. You remember Bethany from the commune? It turned out she quit right after me."

It was hard to admit her failure to her grandparents, who were beaming at her out of her laptop screen. They'd raised her, given her their best. "I just wanted..." Her voice broke. "I just wanted you to be proud of me."

"We *are* proud of you, sweetheart," her grandmother said.

"But...but management won. And Philip, the worst abuser, nearly won the day."

"We're still proud of you," her grandfather said. "You did what you thought was right. You helped people, honey."

"I helped management!"

"No, you helped Houghton and Bethany," her grandmother said. "They're people, too."

Her grandfather nodded. "You helped people, not the company or the bottom line."

"But even that doesn't matter," her grandmother said. "We're proud of you, sweetheart, whatever you decide to do. We're proud of you because we love you."

*

A week later, Edie was sitting at her kitchen table, going through the stack of open positions that she'd printed out. Bethany was with her, making coffee.

Edie's pencil hovered over the programmer's job she had interviewed for yesterday. It was a nice place, progressive and welcoming. But the CEO's hair was too light, and a bit shorter than she trusted...oh heck. She was thinking of Everett again.

Why hadn't he called?

Well, she knew why. He'd basically told her that she was trouble, trouble he didn't need and didn't want. She didn't blame him. After all, who had been Sedgwick's willing fool?

She crossed out the job listing, harder than was necessary.

"Did they offer you a job?" Bethany set a mug of latte in front of Edie and sat next to her with her own mug.

"Yes. But it wasn't quite right." Edie sipped. The sting of caffeine mingled with chocolate and sweet creamer. After a profitless week of searching and more than a little blue, Edie was very glad Bethany and her espresso machine had come to visit. "So far five companies have. None of them were quite right. You?"

"I've got two interviews tomorrow."

"Good work." Edie paused. "I've been wanting to ask something. Why did you quit HHE? You'd just been promoted."

"The rumors." Bethany shuddered. "Houghie, thanks to you, is starting to see me as a force in my own right. But even he believed I got the HHE promotion because we were sleeping together. I quit because I need a job of my own, Edie. Something I can be proud of, that Houghie can be proud of me for having."

Edie thought of her grandparents, who were proud of her just because they loved her, and rubbed suddenly itchy eyes. Apparently, Howell wasn't like that. Yet.

Everett was.

A tear squeezed out. She dashed it away.

"Thinking about Everett?"

"Could you tell?" She tried to take her mind off him by doodling on the job listings. "He hasn't called."

"And you can't call him?" Bethany asked dryly.

"Oh, I called. Once." Up the P, down the R, circle the O… "He was distracted. Said he's in the middle of setting something up, and that he'd call when he was done. But he hasn't. I've wanted to call him, but what if that was really a brush off?" She focused on the listing she'd traced. *Programming manager wanted.*

"Then he's an idiot," Bethany said. "Get on with your life, Edie. Get a kick-ass job. Then call him and make him beg."

"Kick-ass job?" Edie picked up the paper. "Listen to this. Small but growing company. Employee-centered management style a must. Position may work closely with president. And the salary is definitely kick-ass."

"Employee-centered? That sounds like just your thing." Bethany leaned over. "Holy mama."

"What?"

"That's Tarcorp Consulting. They're *the* up and comer. Investors clamoring to drown them in cash, full of bleeding-edge technology, *and* they're great to their employees. Well? What are you waiting for? Call them." Bethany grabbed Edie's wrist, so tight it pinched. "And I want in."

"Ouch, okay." Edie punched the number into her phone. She gave the smooth contralto at the other end her name and some of her qualifications.

The woman asked a few questions, then said, "You sound like just the person we need, Ms. Rowan. Could you come tomorrow for an interview?"

Edie gave Bethany a thumbs up. "I could come in today."

"Wonderful! We have an opening in an hour, at ten. And another at eleven. Would either of those work?"

Bethany grabbed her wrist again. Edie ground molars through the pain. "Well, actually...I know another progressive manager who'd be great. Could we have both appointments?"

"Absolutely. See you at ten."

Edie clicked off. "We're in. Can you let me go now?"

Bethany squealed and swept Edie into a hug that was actually more painful than the snake bite. "Thank you, thank you! This is ten times better than HHE. Houghie'll just puke with envy. I've got interview clothes in the car. Can I—?"

"Bathroom's yours." Released, Edie raced into her bedroom, sloughed sweats and donned heels and hose. They made it to Tarcorp Consulting with five minutes to spare.

The place had an attractive setup, half open, half private offices, and plenty of sunlight and lovely plants and art. The dozen people visible were in various stages of working, including two unabashedly doing nothing but thinking.

The receptionist guided them to the back. "Ms. Blondelle, you're scheduled with HR, that door there. Ms. Rowan, you'll interview with the president first." She gestured Edie into a sunny corner office.

The office was split into two sections, a large sitting area with couches and tables, and a work area.

Behind the workstation, chestnut hair falling in loose waves to his shoulders, was Edward Everett Kirk.

Edie slowed. He looked up.

Their eyes met.

A smile spread on his face, brighter than the sunlight streaming through the windows. "Edie, right on time." Without embarrassment, he leaped to his feet and hugged her.

"Have a nice interview." The receptionist grinned and left.

Everett waved Edie to the couches. "I was going to call you tomorrow. Your timing is perfect. As usual."

She stumbled to a couch and sat. "You started your own company, Mr. Kirk?"

"Restarted. Seemed like the best fit for me. Combines my corporate know-how with the independence of my Tarzan. I'm Everett here, not Mr. Kirk." His smile grew.

Edie got lost in that dimple. She missed him so badly she shook with it.

He sat beside her, took her hands in his. "Edie, I'm sorry. I should have seen Sedgwick was behind the trouble at HHE sooner. I would have, but I was so angry and heartsick after your hearing. Then, when I figured it out, I was furious with myself for letting him get the upper hand. I was so afraid he'd threaten you before I could take him out."

Her heart warmed, hearing that. "He was tricky, Everett. I let him use me, not once, but twice."

"He deceived you. That's different. Then, after he was arrested, well…I couldn't face you until I had fixed it so I'd never be that vulnerable again. So that *you* would never be vulnerable again. I'd started my own company years ago and decided to spin it up again, expand it."

"But you didn't call." Her fears bubbled out. "It was a *week*. You could have told me."

"I didn't want to call until I was sure I could make a go of it. But I couldn't have waited much longer. I missed you so much." He smiled. "Forgive me?"

She'd been so worried, but she couldn't lie to him. Never could. She smiled back. "Always."

They smiled for long moments into each other's eyes. Then Everett cleared his throat. "Let me tell you about the position

I've got in mind for you. A people manager. Someone who can relate to the worker, and fights for the little guy. Someone who complements both my Tarzan and my Kirk." He kissed her hand. "The job title is Partner."

She clasped his hands like a lifeline. "What about fraternization between employees?"

"I hope so." He released her with one hand to snag a box out of his pants pocket. A ring box. "I love you, Edith Ellen Rowan. I hope you'll say yes to a lifetime partnership, in business and at home."

"Oh, Everett, I love you too. Yes!"

To: ED@mythicmail.com
From: ThePrez@serenityrangers.com
Subject: I love you

Edie—I love you too :)
—Everett

About the Author

I live in the Midwest with my beta-reader husband, two grandcats who demand equal lap time, a basement full of spare computer parts, and several musical instruments including a romantic cello and a flute for playing orchestral twittering birds. Visit me at *www.maryhughesbooks.com*, Facebook MaryHughesAuthor, or Twitter @MaryHughesBooks. I'd love to hear from you! Write me at mary@maryhughesbooks.com.

In the mood for more Crimson Romance? Check out *Wildly* by Debra Kayn at CrimsonRomance.com.